W9-CIL-269

GORDON KORMAN
NO COINS, PLEASE

GORDON KORMAN
NO COINS, PLEASE

Cover by Richard Williams

Scholastic-TAB Publications, Ltd.
123 Newkirk Road, Richmond Hill, Ontario, Canada

Canadian Cataloguing in Publication Data

    Korman, Gordon.
       No coins, please

    ISBN 0-590-71444-9

    I. Title.

    PS8571.078N6 1984a   jC813′.54   C84-098586-X
    PZ7.K67No 1984a

1st printing 1984   **Printed in Hong Kong by Everbest Printers**

For Howard Newman,
the original cross-country counselor

Contents

Contents

The Ambulance

Rob Nevin looked from his friend to the application form on the table between them and back to his friend again.

"You're kidding."

Dennis Leaver grinned broadly. "No. It's a great idea." From his pocket he produced a colorful brochure and placed it in front of Rob. "Here, look at this."

Rob frowned. *"Juniortours: Fun, Education and Adventure wrapped up in an exciting trip your youngster will never forget.* Come on! You want us to be counselors on this thing?"

Dennis pointed to a picture of two stalwart counselors standing behind six bright-eyed young boys, all of them framed by the Grand Canyon and an immaculately blue sky. "That's us in a few weeks."

"But, Dennis, we'll have kids to take care of. We don't know anything about kids."

Dennis shrugged. "What's to know? You just drive them around and make sure they don't get

1

themselves killed. That's all there is to it. And we get an all-expense-paid trip from Montreal to Los Angeles in our own van. We even get paid for it."

Rob snorted. "Five hundred dollars isn't exactly what I'd call big bucks for five weeks' work. We could make a lot more than that sweeping floors or something. I've got a line on jobs as painters' assistants for us. I'm supposed to let the guy know some time this week."

"Tell him no deal. We're traveling men. If we took that painting job we'd never get out of Montreal all summer. We're going to see the world, not the inside of some Côte St. Luc living room-dining room. Besides, we'll get tips. At the end of the tour all the grateful parents slip the counselors a little something extra."

"It's what they slip you at the beginning of the trip that worries me—their kids."

"Here. Let me read you what it says: *Last year Juniortours fielded one hundred vans, criss-crossing the continental United States on seven different routes, carrying six hundred boys and girls.* You hear that, Nevin? Boys and *girls*. That means there are female counselors. Are there any female painters?"

Rob hesitated. "Well . . . "

"Not to mention all the girls we'll meet just as a matter of course on the trip. We'll be staying over long enough in some places to get to know people. Look at this—first stop, New York. *New York,* Nevin. As soon as we get the kids off to sleep, the whole city will be there at our feet!"

"Come on, Dennis!" Rob exclaimed. "You talk

2

like we're driving cabbages here. These are kids. They get stomach aches, they get lonely, they throw up, they cry, they wet their beds!"

"Don't be silly. These aren't babies. The youngest they'll be is eleven. Think back to when you were eleven. You didn't do any of those things. Eleven-year-olds are men." He laughed delightedly. "The whole thing is fantastic—so fantastic it almost makes me wonder if there's a catch."

"According to this brochure," said Rob sourly, "there are six catches per van. Dennis, come on. Take the painting job with me."

"And this is a golden opportunity too, because they've never had any Canadian kids on the tour before. We'll be ambassadors of good will."

"We'll be nursemaids."

"I told you, these kids are men. Here, the application's all filled out except for your signature. Uh—I took the liberty of adding a few years' experience in a day-care center to your life. A little dishonest, maybe, but we don't want to miss out on this."

"Oh, and what did you put in your own résumé? You're a well-known pediatrician, I suppose?"

"Just a few years as a camp counselor." Dennis grinned smugly. "We're a cinch."

Rob leapt to his feet. "I wouldn't get involved in this thing if there was no painter's job and I had to spend the summer lying on the cedar deck rotting and fighting with the mosquitoes for my own blood! You're crazy!"

Dennis looked concerned. "You know, if we don't get our applications in on time we might not make it."

"Forget it, Dennis! No way!"

* * *

Through the Montreal traffic moved a shiny white van, the flashy *J.T.* Juniortours logo splashed in red and yellow on its side. It jerked and balked as it turned a corner.

"Ah, Nevin, my boy, you'll never regret this," said Dennis, shifting gears. Loud screeches of protest issued from the engine. "This is going to be the trip of a lifetime."

"I can tell," said Rob sourly, jamming his baseball cap further down over his curly dark hair. "Can't you manage a smoother ride, or are we going to bounce all the way to California?"

"I'm getting the hang of it," said Dennis cheerfully. "I just can't wait to meet the guys."

Rob moaned. His protests and refusals had all come to nothing, withering under the fire of his best friend's enthusiasm. He had cracked under the promise of the open road, city lights, the great outdoors, the California sun and hordes of beautiful women. He hated himself for it, but he had traded his paintbrush for a clipboard with six names and addresses on it—his charges-to-be.

With a grinding of gears they rounded a corner and pulled to a halt in front of the first house on the list. Dennis took an instant liking to Sheldon, greeting him like a long-lost son and jabbering ecstatically about the wonderful time in store. Sheldon, however, didn't appear to be paying attention—he kept his mournful brown eyes trained on his

4

shoelaces and his conversation restricted to "yes" and "no" answers. His mind was obviously elsewhere, but this didn't seem to bother Dennis. For his part, Rob was friendly and tried to look reasonably optimistic about the trip.

With Sheldon and his gear loaded into the van, they proceeded to the next address to pick up Howie, a tall, thin, blond boy with glasses and an endearing, slightly goofy smile. Howie, Rob reflected, was the sort of person who would go through life being liked, and Dennis, of course, was duly impressed.

The next stop added Nick to the roster. Nick seemed very excited about the trip, but he didn't feel up to facing the open road without his rabbit's foot. This sparked a lively debate between the boy and his parents, in which Dennis acted as self-appointed mediator, until it was finally agreed that the rabbit's foot could go. Nick, his round face beaming, was then loaded into the van under Dennis's approving eye.

Kevin, next on the list, was a dark boy, small for his age. He was all business, though, and paid almost no attention to his mother, but kept himself occupied with directing Dennis and Rob in the loading and placement of his camera equipment. A large tripod, a camera bag, two cases of lenses and filters, and an enormous duffle bag marked *film* accompanied his small suitcase of clothing. Only when the packing was done to his satisfaction did he exchange a fond farewell with his anxious mother, and the group headed on.

Next came Sam, who looked like the perfect kid.

Clear-eyed, dark-haired and athletic, he seemed ready to take on the world with a devil-may-care style which he had long worked on. He suffered a temporary loss of image when his mother kissed him goodbye, but with help from Dennis he managed to carry it off rather well.

By this point, Dennis's enchantment with his group had grown almost to the point of rapture.

"We are definitely the luckiest counselors on the whole tour!" he yodeled gleefully as they made their way towards the last address on the list. "You guys just get acquainted with each other. We've got one more pick-up, then on to New York!"

There was restrained cheering from the five, which Rob interpreted as excitement over the trip mixed with misgivings about leaving home.

The final stop was a large, attractive brick house in the heart of suburbia. "Hi, Mrs. Geller," Dennis greeted the woman who answered the door. "I'm Dennis from Juniortours, and this is my partner, Rob. We've come to pick up Arthur."

She ushered them into the front hall, and Rob watched his friend's eyes for the look of loving welcome signifying that Arthur measured up to the perfection of the five they had left waiting in the van.

"Artie, the van is here." Mrs. Geller disappeared for a moment and returned with a slim, dark boy dressed much as the others had been in jeans and a T-shirt, except that around his neck he wore a small leather pouch suspended on a stout string. Over his shoulder was slung a large duffle bag, and in his right hand he carried a black leather attaché case with the letter *A* engraved on the lock.

Dennis chortled with delight. "Hi there, Artie. All ready to go, I see. I'm Dennis, and this is Rob."

"Have you packed everything on the check list, Mrs. Geller?" Rob asked politely.

"Oh, yes."

"And Artie has his spending money?" Dennis prompted.

She flushed slightly. "Well, he has a few dollars. It's enough."

Dennis's earnest face grew grave. "Well, the tour's recommended amount is seventy-five dollars, and all the other boys have at least that much. We wouldn't want Artie to be left out of anything."

Mrs. Geller hesitated. "Well, sometimes it's not such a good idea to let Artie have too much money, because—"

"Oh, I see." Dennis smiled knowingly. "Don't worry. We won't let him spend it foolishly."

She sighed. "Well, I suppose seventy-five dollars isn't too much money if you hold it for him. You will watch him very closely, won't you?"

"Scout's honor," Dennis beamed, accepting the crisp bills. "All right, Artie, let's hit the road." Dennis grabbed Artie's duffle bag and Rob reached for the attaché case.

"Oh, I can carry this," said Artie casually. He turned to his mother. "Goodbye, Mom. I'll write."

She kissed him soundly on the cheek. "You'll be good, like you promised Dad and me?"

Artie nodded.

"Don't worry, Mrs. Geller," said Dennis. "Artie'll be just fine."

"Be good," she repeated, and continued to call out the same two words as she stood on the front lawn watching the van pull away.

"Your mom seems a little nervous," Rob commented.

"Oh, it's okay," said Artie in his soft voice. "She's just a little overprotective."

"All right, guys, this is just great!" Dennis raved. "We're going to be the best group Juniortours ever had!"

There was dead silence.

Rob looked back. "Uh—Dennis," he whispered, "I hate to tell you this, but three of your men are crying."

Dennis glanced in the rear-view mirror. Sheldon, Kevin and Nick were all in tears, and Howie wore a long, forlorn face. "Aw, come on, guys," he wheedled. "Don't be sad. I know it's kind of a drag to be away from home for the first time, but we're going to have a ball together. Right, Rob?"

"Sure," said Rob with as much conviction as he could muster.

"Besides, we've got a lot of important business to take care of before we get to New York," Dennis went on. "We need a name for our van. It has to be a great name, too, because that's what we're going to be called when all the different groups meet up at the check-points along the way. Maybe we should be something fearsome, like the Monsters."

Someone in the back seat honked into a handkerchief.

"Not so good, eh?" said Dennis. "Well, what do you guys think?"

Sheldon perked up. "I saw a movie once where the hero named his van Old Betsy."

"Are you nuts?" cried Sam. "Do you want to jog onto a soccer field while they announce us as Betsy?"

Kevin looked thoughtful. "Well, we're traveling around a lot, so why don't we call ourselves the Rovers?"

"Forget it," said Howie. "That's what you call a dog."

"I know!" said Nick. "We'll be the Horseshoes, for luck."

"How about you, Artie?" piped Dennis. "Any ideas?"

Artie, sitting with his attaché case on his lap, shrugged casually. "Whatever you guys come up with will be just fine, I'm sure."

"Uh—yeah," said Dennis. "These are all great suggestions, but I kind of pictured something a little more unique, you know, something that reflects the van. Like White Lightning or the White Tornado."

Rob laughed mirthlessly. "White Lightning? If you want a good name for a white van, try the Ambulance."

A big cheer went up from the back.

"Perfect!" exclaimed Sam. "The Ambulance!"

"I love it!" Nick decided.

"Aw, come on, guys," Dennis protested. "You don't want to be the Ambulance. It's silly."

"We can have a group yell!" exclaimed Kevin. He opened his mouth and emitted the piercing scream of an ambulance siren. Sam and Nick joined in with enthusiasm.

"We've got the best name on the whole tour!" crowed Howie. "Thanks, Rob."

"Don't mention it," Rob grinned, enjoying the look of dismay on Dennis's face.

"But guys, not the Ambulance—"

"Oh yes, it's perfect," said Sam with great authority. "Everyone else is going to have a boring name like the Wanderers."

"How unoriginal," said Howie, nodding wisely.

"The Ambulance is—you know—creative," said Sam. "We'll be one of a kind."

"Way to go, Nevin," muttered Dennis bitterly. "We've got the dumbest name on the whole tour, and it's all your fault."

Rob shrugged, grinning. "You wanted to be unique."

* * *

As the day's driving progressed and the boys chatted among themselves and with their counselors, one thing became apparent to Rob. Sheldon could fill in any space in a conversation, and was more than willing to do so.

"My best friend in the world is Pete Ogrodnick," he was saying. "The Ogrodnicks live around the corner on Elm Street, right next to the plaza with the bake shop where Pete and I used to go for chocolate fudge cookies. They were so good I can almost taste them now ..."

Rob glanced back to see that the five other boys had tuned Sheldon out and were looking absently out the windows. Dennis was not listening either, although he was trying to appear attentive by nodding his head at intervals and uttering the occasional "Uh huh."

"Pete's twenty-one now. He was ten when I was born, but that never stopped us from being good friends. He even tried to teach me to ride a bike. He put in a lot of time before we gave up. Pete says I'm unco-ordinated, but he says it with love." Sheldon's face turned tragic. "I'll bet he can't get those great fudge cookies in Helsinki."

"Pete moved away, did he?" said Rob, almost comatose.

"Yeah. All the way to Finland. He's working at the shipyards there, installing telephones on this new cruise ship, the *Lady Jane*. Pete says the *Lady Jane* has a hundred and sixty-seven telephones. Pete's the greatest guy in the world."

"I think I have to go to the bathroom," announced Kevin.

"Yeah, I think we could all use a pit stop," Dennis agreed. "We'll pull in at the next service area."

Sheldon was still talking, not missing a beat. "Pete and I had some great times together. I'll never forget the time we . . . "

* * *

The white van was at rest in a trailer camp just north of New York City. The canvas shelter concealed in its roof had been pulled out and down, and the six boys lay sleeping in their bedrolls on the ground sheet under it.

The day's driving had ended well after dark, and

11

they had checked into the camp in order to give the boys a good night's sleep before the big Juniortours opening meeting in Central Park the next morning. The two counselors, however, were still awake after midnight, seated at a picnic table examining a small slip of paper by flashlight.

"I still say we should plead 'not guilty,'" said Dennis peevishly. "There's no way I was driving sixty-seven miles an hour."

"How can we plead 'not guilty'? We can't come back from wherever we are to appear in court in upstate New York. We have to plead guilty and pay the fine."

Dennis looked disgusted. "This is justice?" He filled in the traffic citation, added *The radar must have been defective,* and signed it. "We can mail it tomorrow."

"Just be grateful the officer believed us about not being able to hear his siren because of the group yell. It's a good thing he took *Gave chase* off his report, or we'd be in jail right now."

"Don't blame our guys," said Dennis protectively, addressing and sealing the envelope. "That whole thing's your fault anyway. The Ambulance!" He affixed a stamp. "You know, Juniortours is going to be really upset about having to pay this ticket."

"Why should they have to pay it?" Rob demanded. "You were driving."

Dennis dealt him a withering glare which lost some of its bite because of the dim light. "You, the genius, have just explained that we're going to be on the road. Where will they be able to reach me except at the Juniortours office?"

"*Excuse* me," said Rob.

Dennis put the envelope in his pocket and stretched. "You know," he said reflectively, "if we didn't have such a great time ahead of us this could have been a really lousy day. Well, I'm not going to let a little speeding ticket ruin my vacation. And tomorrow morning I'll talk the guys out of this Ambulance bit, and everything'll be cool. Didn't we get a great bunch of kids?"

"They're okay, I suppose. Not exactly what I'd call men, though. I'm not so thrilled with the idea that when we got Sheldon we also got saddled with the ghost of Pete Ogrodnick. 'Pete says, Pete says.' I hate the guy and I've never even met him. If we have to listen to Ogrodnick lore all the way to California I'm going to shoot myself right now."

"Sheldon's okay," said Dennis.

"And that Artie kind of worries me. His mother seemed awfully concerned about him being good. I think that means he's usually bad."

"Nevin, you amaze me. Can't you see that Artie is the most harmless kid in the world? He said himself his mother was overprotective. That's the whole problem. Obviously he's been overpowered by his family for so long that he doesn't even have a word to say for himself. That's why it's our responsibility as his counselors to bring him out of his shell and let him develop an identity and a sense of self-esteem. This trip is going to be the turning point of his whole life."

"Okay, professor," said Rob. "Does your psychoanalysis explain that briefcase of his—the one he takes to the bathroom and is presently sleeping with? And how about the leather pouch around his neck?"

"He's probably got a good luck piece in there," said Dennis. "And the briefcase is maybe just a little quirk. Don't worry. When we get through with him Artie'll be a new man."

Rob frowned. "So I suppose both our lives are now dedicated to the rehabilitation of Artie Geller."

Dennis grinned knowingly. "I know what you're getting at. Don't panic. Tomorrow morning in Central Park we get our first chance to scout out the female half of this tour. There'll be plenty of time in the next five weeks for both the kids *and* the ladies."

14

Where's Artie?

Charlie Butcher, executive tour director of Juniortours Inc., stood at the podium on the Great Lawn of Central Park in New York City. The hot July sun shone down on the fifty vans before him. Campers and counselors were assembled in front of their vehicles, waiting for the official start of the tour.

"All right, attention, everybody!" Butcher barked into the microphone in a voice that boomed across the park. "Hi, there!"

A loud answering "Hi!" echoed his greeting.

"Welcome all you Juniortourists." It was a speech he'd been giving for the past five years, and he closed his mind to it and rambled on. He liked speeches only slightly more than he liked children, which was not very much at all. "You're all very lucky people, because you're going to be driving all the way across this great country." He could not quite conceal his cringe of distaste. Thank heaven Juniortours had a private plane for his personal use, he thought, since there was nothing he hated more

15

than driving. "This is a special year for Juniortours because this year we've got kids coming down from Canada. Right now there are groups here from Montreal and Toronto, and at the big western meeting in Los Angeles there are people from Vancouver—wherever that is. Anyway, you kids are participating in an international event. Now, you're going to keep meeting up with each other at the check-points, so even though we're a big group, we all want to get to know each other. I've got here the list of all the group names from when you checked in. When I call out your name, everybody stand up and scream and wave and be seen." Butcher took a deep breath. This was the part he hated worst of all. "From Farmingdale, New York, the Knights of the Road." Wild cheering came from six campers and their counselors beside a red van.

In the midst of the crowd Dennis turned to Rob. "Well, that's it. We're going to be the laughingstock of Central Park. When he calls out the Ambulance I'm going to go hide in the van."

For the first time Rob was playing with the idea of enjoying himself on the tour. "There are a lot of nice looking girls here."

Dennis nodded sadly. "Wait till they hear the name of our group, Nevin. They'll think we're idiots."

Rob shrugged. "You heard Sam this morning. If you change the name of the group they're going to protest. Besides, so what if we're the Ambulance? Who cares?"

Butcher's voice rang out. "From Montreal, Canada, the—*Ambulance?* What kind of a—?"

16

He was interrupted by the Ambulance group yell. Everyone stared at the wailing campers and their white van, and then waves of laughter swept the clearing.

"It's the best name!" crowed Howie. "Everyone loves it!"

"You see?" said Sam. "I was right."

Dennis studied the grass, his fair complexion flaming.

Rob laughed. All the boys seemed exhilarated, with the exception of Artie, who sat on the ground clutching his attaché case, his expression distant.

Butcher looked disgusted. "All right, pipe down, everybody. We've just got a few more, then we'll hand out the stencils and the paint and you can all put the group names on the vans."

Dennis turned pale.

* * *

While Charlie Butcher's assistants treated three hundred campers to a barbecue lunch, Butcher himself was addressing their counselors in an isolated corner of the park.

"In less than an hour we're turning you loose with our kids. Most companies would have a lot of rules and regulations. I only have one and this is it: everything has to be *perfect*."

There was an uncomfortable murmur.

"Perfect," Butcher repeated. "By this I mean that you're going to follow your schedule exactly and get to the check-points on time. You're going to stay within your budget, and the supplies we give you are going to be exactly the right amount, so there shouldn't be any need for extra spending of tour money. You're going to keep your kids happy and healthy, so they've got no gripes when they get home. Most important of all, there's one word I never want to hear—'lost.' Don't lose anything or anybody, and don't show up somewhere late and tell me you got lost. If you lose so much as a hubcap, you're dead."

He took a deep breath and went on. "Now, Juniortours has offices all over the country and each one's got an emergency number. You've all got a list of those numbers and I've only got one rule about them: don't phone. There's nothing I hate worse than hearing that red telephone ring. It means that everything isn't perfect."

Butcher favored them with a genial smile. "Here's a piece of friendly advice. In my experience at Juniortours, the biggest pains in the neck come when you counselors let the campers out of your sight for even two seconds. So watch them. That's all. Have a good trip."

The counselors scrambled over to the barbecue, anxious to be out of Butcher's presence and eager to keep their charges under surveillance as per instructions. Dennis and Rob found their group happily munching hamburgers.

"Great food!" approved Sam. "We saved you each a burger."

"Thanks." Dennis accepted his lunch and looked around. There were Sam, Howie, Sheldon, Nick, Kevin and—"Where's Artie?"

"Oh, he left," said Sheldon, his mouth full.

Rob choked. "What do you mean, 'left'?"

"Well, he ate fast and said he was going into town," said Howie. "We asked where, and he said nowhere much."

"He said not to worry," Kevin added, "and that he'll meet us back here later. Oh, yeah, and he said to tell you he took his spending money out of the Ambulance. I wonder where he went."

Rob's mind flew back to Butcher's speech. "Oh no, Dennis, he's"—he looked around furtively and dropped his voice to a whisper—"lost!"

"All right, nobody panic," said Dennis shakily. "We're going to take care of this situation efficiently and calmly. We'll find him."

"Where are we going to find him? There are eight million people in New York! Butcher's going to kill us!"

"You don't have to find him," Nick pointed out reasonably. "He's coming back here when he's through. At least, that's what he said."

"Okay," said Dennis. "One of us will take the guys around the city—six heads are better than one —and we'll look for Artie. The other one will stay here in case he comes back."

"But—"

Dennis took out a quarter. "Call it."

"Uh—heads."

The coin flipped and fell. "Tails. Too bad. All right, we'll be back. You wait here."

"But—"

"All right, guys. Into the van."

The last sound Rob heard as the van pulled out

of view was the Ambulance group yell and the screech of gears as Dennis shifted into second.

* * *

The afternoon dragged slowly on. The Juniortours vans pulled out one by one, leaving Rob sitting cross-legged on the Great Lawn of Central Park. His thoughts were in turmoil. The trip hadn't even started and already they had lost a kid. Dennis's "most harmless kid in the world" had disappeared.

There was something strange about Artie. There *was*. Rob had felt it from the beginning. What if he didn't come back? Or worse, what if something happened to him? He was only eleven years old. Where could he be in the vast city? Where?

He'd call Butcher—the emergency line. Surely the disappearance of one of the kids was reason enough —or was it? He recalled Butcher's speech, so fresh in his mind: "Don't phone."

Rob sighed glumly. He never should have signed up for this miserable trip. Why did he always let Dennis talk him into things? He was a victim of his own weakness, and these were the rewards of wishy-washiness. He was responsible for losing an innocent child in New York.

On the other hand, the "innocent child" had taken off on his own, attaché case in hand, without telling anyone where he was going or what he planned to do there. Not only that, but he had appropriated seventy-five dollars without permission. The money was his, but still . . .

20

"What am I going to do?" Rob cried aloud.

A passing roller skater shrugged expressively and moved on.

Rob lay back in despair. He watched the clouds for a while, but then the late night and early rising caught up with him and he fell fast asleep.

* * *

"Rob. Rob, wake up." Rob awoke to see Artie Geller peering mildly down at him. He sat bolt upright and grabbed the boy by the shirt.

"Artie, where were you? Where have you been?"

Artie shrugged. "Oh—nowhere."

"Everyone's searching the streets of New York for you," said Rob angrily. He looked at his watch. "It's quarter to six! You're in big trouble, mister!"

"Why?" asked Artie innocently.

"Well, because you left without telling anybody."

"I told everybody who was there."

"And you took money without permission. That's stealing!"

Artie looked surprised. "The money was mine."

"But your mother gave it to us to hold for you. Hand it over."

Artie reached into his pocket and produced a dime and a nickel.

"Fifteen cents!" Rob was appalled. "Where's the other $74.85?"

"I spent it."

"You spent it? On what? What do you have to show for that money? Not so much as a lollipop!"

"Don't worry," said Artie gravely. "I didn't spend it foolishly."

"But we made a promise to your mother that we'd watch your money, and because of you we've let her down."

Artie shrugged. "She gave it to you to hold until I needed it, and I needed it today."

"For what? To throw into some video game? Now you're not going to have any money left for the whole trip."

Artie said nothing.

"Well, you sit right down here beside me and don't move a muscle. We're going to wait for the van to get back. Dennis and the other guys aren't going to be too pleased with you, ruining their whole day!"

The two sat, Rob seething with indignation, Artie serene, cradling his briefcase lovingly in his arms. It was forty-five minutes before the van came to pick them up.

The air rang with the horn and the Ambulance group yell as the white van drove up the pathway and stopped. Rob stared in amazement as the six passengers disembarked. Dennis was splendid in an I♥NY T-shirt, a garishly-studded belt and an enormous sombrero fringed with velvet pom-poms.

"Oh, hi, Artie, glad you're back. Boy, Rob, you missed out on a great day."

Rob was trembling with rage. "Dennis, what kind of counselor are you anyway? When you left here six hours ago we were missing a kid! And you went on a pleasure jaunt and left me to cope with the whole thing!"

Dennis paused. "Well, Artie's here, so we must have done something right, eh? Anyway, we saw everything! Right, guys?"

"Right," said Sam. "My favorite part was when we ran out of gas on that big wide street right in the middle of rush hour."

Nick giggled. "Yeah, Fifth Avenue. Everyone was shouting and honking their horns, and then the policeman went right up to Dennis and said, 'Move out, idiot.' It was great!"

Kevin patted his 35-mm camera. "I got a close-up of his face! What a shot! In the bottom corner you'll see him shaking his fist at Dennis!"

"And anyway," Dennis went on, "while we were walking around with our bucket looking for a gas station we bought all this great stuff."

Tearing his eyes from Dennis, Rob noted that the five campers were similarly decorated with tourist paraphernalia. "Well, I'm glad to see you all spent money. Artie spent a little money today too. Seventy-five dollars."

"Yeah?" asked Dennis excitedly. "What'd you get?"

Artie shrugged. "Nothing special."

Rob clenched his fists in exasperation. "Dennis, I want to talk to you!"

"Sure, but first let's get to the campsite and fix something to eat. We're all starved. Come on, everybody. All aboard." As he and Rob climbed into the front seat he added, "New place tonight. Some park in Long Island where a lot of the tour groups are staying. They're probably all eating already." He looked vaguely annoyed. "We could be too if we hadn't had to pick you guys up."

Rob bit his tongue and said nothing.

* * *

The trailer park was largely populated by Junior-tours vans, since about half the New York contingent was stationed there. By eleven o'clock all of the campers were asleep under their protective tent flaps, but some of the counselors remained awake. Dennis and Rob sat on the grass in front of their van.

"Finally they're asleep," Dennis was saying. "I didn't think Sheldon would ever shut up. I've never seen such a happy bunch of kids in my life."

"I'm miserable enough to cancel out their happiness," Rob growled.

"Gee, I'm really sorry about that, but we drove all around New York, and when we didn't see Artie we figured he was with you. So we went sightseeing."

"But what about his money, Dennis? It's all gone. He went out with seventy-five bucks and came back with fifteen cents."

Dennis shrugged. "So he'll learn a valuable lesson when he wants something and can't afford it. We're here to educate as well, you know. And from time to time we'll stake him a few dollars to see that he has a good time too."

Rob sighed. "I guess you're right. But that kid worries me. You can't get a straight answer out of him. No matter how hard we tried—me, you, the other kids—he wouldn't tell us where he went today

24

or what he spent that money on."

Dennis yawned. "He's probably just ashamed. See, he's learning the lesson already. Hey, I didn't tell you what happened today. I met this really nice girl on the street. All the guys insisted we take turns carrying the gas, and Sheldon spilled some all over this really nice girl's shoes. So I struck up a conversation. She's an NYU student majoring in drama. I was going to ask for her phone number, but I didn't feel the moment was right."

Rob laughed. "Probably because she was ready to take off her shoe, stuff it in your mouth and light it. You know, Dennis, since you've got so much experience as a ladies' man, maybe we should go over and say hello to those two Boston girls, the Pink Panthers. They're sitting there all alone."

Dennis snuck a furtive glance. "They do look kind of nice. Of course, when we introduce ourselves as the Ambulance it's all over."

Rob nonchalantly craned his neck and snuck another look. "Come on, Dennis. What's in a name?"

"Okay, but give me a minute to get psyched up. And don't look at them so obviously. They'll think we're idiots."

The two boys sat there for a moment staring straight ahead. While Dennis prepared himself mentally and Rob searched his mind for casual opening remarks, the counselors from the Road Hogs, a van based in Bridgeport, Connecticut, walked over and introduced themselves to the girls. By the time Dennis and Rob turned their gaze back in the direction of Boston an amiable conversation was already in progress.

Dennis was incensed. "The nerve of those guys, moving in on our territory!"

"Oh, shut up, Dennis—let's get some sleep."

* * *

"Well, guys," said Dennis, leading the Ambulance group out of the Empire State Building towards Avenue of the Americas, "wasn't that an amazing view?"

"It sure was!" exclaimed Sam. "Right, guys?"

"Right!"

"I can tell you enjoyed it, Artie," Dennis went on. "We almost had to pry you away from those binoculars with a crowbar. What was so fascinating down there?"

Artie looked vague. "Oh—nothing. Cities are interesting."

Dennis nudged Rob. "You see?" he whispered. "He's learned his lesson already. The problem with you, Nevin, is you have no faith in human nature." Aloud, he announced, "All right, guys, next stop—Times Square!"

The boys stirred with excitement and the whole group started walking a little faster, except for Artie, who gradually began to lag to the rear. The others strode down the street, absorbed by their surroundings. Just past a subway entrance they turned onto Avenue of the Americas and began to walk uptown.

A few minutes passed. A head emerged cautiously from the subway entrance, eyes searching the street.

Artie Geller, immaculate in a black tuxedo with satin lapels, black tie and cummerbund accenting a snowy white frilled shirt and spotless white gloves, slipped up the stairs and began to walk purposefully down the street.

His first stop was an establishment on Broadway, one of the places he had visited the day before, Quick-Print Small Printing Jobs. With a neat parcel under his arm he proceeded to Katz's Kustom Kontainers and picked up two cartons. Another parcel awaited him at a leather goods shop a little way down the block. Then he stopped at a grocery store and came out with a giant economy-size jar of grape jelly, a stainless steel spoon and a copy of the *New York Times*.

Slipping into an isolated alleyway he arranged his parcels on the ground and began to open them. He took out thirty little cardboard boxes, three inches by three inches by three inches, and placed them in front of him. Then came thirty one-fluid-ounce glass jars. Each jar received a sticker from the print shop parcel, then was spooned full of grape jelly and sealed. A printed sheet was carefully folded and wrapped around the jar, and both were placed inside the box. Finally, a small rectangular card was added. The contents of the leather goods package were duly distributed, one per unit, and the whole arrangement was topped off by a square of newspaper carefully torn from the *Times*.

Artie closed the lids of the boxes, loaded them into the largest carton and moved to the intersection of Twenty-Third Street and Fifth Avenue, a spot he had selected from the observation deck of the Empire State Building for the quality and quantity of its passing trade.

He emptied the carton, turned it over to use as a table and arranged his stock in a pyramid, opening one box as a display. It took only seconds for a young boy in a tuxedo, obviously open for business, to attract attention. A man in a gray pinstripe three-piece suit ambled over and smiled at Artie.

"That's a nice little monkey suit you've got there, son. What are you selling?"

Wordlessly Artie reached into the box, pulled out the jar and pointed to the sticker. It read: *Attack Jelly.*

The man goggled. "Attack jelly? What's that?"

"Why, protection for your home and loved ones, of course," Artie replied. "You never can be too careful these days."

A look of disbelief came over the customer's face. "Okay, kid, how does it work?"

Artie dismantled the package. "Well, you get your attack jelly and your complete instruction booklet, which includes indoor and outdoor use plus care, grooming and upkeep. And this is the sign for your front door, *These Premises Protected by Attack Jelly,* as a warning to burglars. Then there's the quality leather leash, studded for the stylish look, so you can exercise your jelly, and some newspaper for paper-training. But let me assure you, sir, they train very quickly. The set comes complete for ten dollars. No coins, please."

With effort the man ripped his eyes from the table to stare at Artie. "Ten bucks for a jar of jam? Are you crazy?"

"It's a small price to pay to sleep soundly in your bed at night. And, confidentially, I'm pretty sure you'll get a reduction on your house insurance rates when you tell the company you have attack jelly. All in all, it's a very good investment."

The man stared, then laughed loudly. Bereft of speech, he reached into his wallet, produced a ten-dollar bill and handed it to Artie. "All right, you little bandit," he gasped finally. "I'll take one. It's ridiculous, I know, but for an act like that ... " He looked down the street and waved. "Hey, Fred— Murray—come over here. You've got to see this!"

Attracted by the first customer's roars of mirth a large crowd was gathering, and soon the words "attack jelly" were being passed merrily along the street. Artie was sold out in half an hour, and was on his way with three hundred dollars to visit his suppliers.

* * *

"Hey," said Rob, looking around suddenly. "Where's Artie?"

The group stopped dead on the sidewalk and scanned the area.

"That Artie," said Dennis in perplexity. "I just can't seem to figure him out."

"He's a weird guy!" decided Sam.

"Yeah," said Howie. "He keeps leaving all the time. I guess he doesn't like us very much."

"Come on, guys, don't be like that," Dennis protested. "Artie's just shy—"

"It's a little more complicated than that, Dennis!" cried Rob, feeling the first symptoms of panic assail his system. "That kid is loose in the city with fifteen cents in his pocket!"

"Pete Ogrodnick always says that you should never lose your cool when things go wrong," put in Sheldon.

"That's easy for him to say!" said Rob defensively. "He's safe in Helsinki!"

"All right," Dennis announced, "we've been in this situation before. He was with us just a few minutes ago, so he couldn't have gone far. Let's retrace our steps and look for him."

"Why should we, if he doesn't want to be with us?" put in Nick.

"Because we're a group," argued Dennis, "and we have to stick together. We have to show Artie that we want him."

"Look," said Rob. "We've got to be reasonable about this thing. I don't think we lost Artie. I think Artie lost us."

Dennis looked puzzled. "So what's the difference? We've still got to find him."

"But he's not going to hang around waiting for us to catch him."

"Okay. But we can't just walk around the whole city hoping to run into him. Let's go get the van."

"Oh, no, you don't! I'm not running out of gas on Fifth Avenue in the middle of a crisis. Let's phone Butcher."

Dennis turned pale. "Nevin, are you crazy? Phone on the *emergency line* to give him the word *lost?* He'll kill us! Worse yet, he'll kick us off the tour!"

30

"Why don't we go to Times Square?" Nick suggested. "Artie knew we were going there. If he wants us that's where he'll go too."

"And I can get some good shots," added Kevin, brandishing his camera.

Dennis looked at Rob. "What do you think?"

"I think that's what Pete Ogrodnick would do," confirmed Sheldon.

Rob sighed helplessly. "What have we got to lose?"

They began to make their way northward.

"How about the group yell?" exclaimed Howie.

"Not here," said Sam self-consciously. "It isn't dignified."

* * *

Business was booming at Artie's new location up Fifth Avenue at Forty-Ninth Street. The customers were crowded all around and the new shipment of a hundred boxes was dwindling.

"Yes, they really do become quite affectionate," Artie was telling an executive from NBC. "Of course, they never lose their bite, though. After all, they're for protection first and companionship second."

"Kid, you're crazy. I'll take two."

A younger man held out two five-dollar bills. "I need one for my girlfriend. She's always complaining she needs more locks—now she'll be safe. She'll have attack jelly."

"You're right, sir; they make wonderful gifts," said Artie, accepting the money and handing over a

31

box. "Who's next? Don't crowd, please."

"Kid, who are you working for?" asked a new attack jelly owner.

"Well," Artie replied, "I'm an independently sponsored agent working free-lance for the various attack jelly breeding farms. Thank you, miss. I'm sure your goldfish will be very happy to have company ... "

* * *

Rob looked helplessly around Times Square. "Where is he? It must be five o'clock!"

"Five-o-four and fifty-six seconds," Dennis confirmed. "Fifty-seven, fifty-eight, fifty-nine, five-o-five."

"Dennis, I can't believe you! Artie's missing, and you buy a new watch!"

Dennis looked ashamed. "Sorry, I couldn't pass this up. Thirty-five dollars. It was a steal."

"It probably was, coming from that store, but that's not important. Where's Artie?"

"I don't think he's going to show up," Kevin decided.

"Don't you think I know that?" exclaimed Rob in exasperation. "He doesn't even know where to find us!"

"Maybe he'll go back to where we parked the Ambulance," said Sheldon.

"That's right!" exclaimed Dennis triumphantly. "Okay, guys, back to the Empire State Building. I'll time us with my stop watch."

All seven headed at a brisk trot down to the spot where they had left the van several hours earlier. A shiny gray Rolls Royce sat in the space where the white Juniortours van had once been.

"It's gone!" gasped Rob. "It was right here, and it's gone!"

Dennis knocked politely on the window of the Rolls, and the smoked glass receded quietly into the door. A uniformed chauffeur peered out questioningly. "Excuse me, sir," said Dennis, "but have you seen a white van? Uh—it was parked here before."

The chauffeur sniffed. "I have not actually seen your vehicle, but I should imagine *that* might provide some clue to its whereabouts." He pointed a gloved finger to a sign which read: *Two-hour Parking Only. Violators Will Be Towed Away At Owner's Expense.* The smoked glass rose again and the chauffeur was gone.

"Oh, no," moaned Rob.

"Our Ambulance!" exclaimed Sam.

"Okay," Dennis decided. "All we have to do is phone and find out where they towed the van, go pick it up, come back here and get Artie. So Rob, you wait here and we'll go for the van."

"Forget it, Dennis. There's no way I'm doing the waiting this time. *You* wait here and *I'll* pick up the van."

"We'll go with Rob," decided Kevin.

As it turned out the van was being held in a large warehouse on Twelfth Avenue, at the very western edge of Manhattan. Rob hailed a cab and bundled himself and his five charges inside. The ride was a costly affair through stop-and-go traffic, and the police warehouse was a dilapidated structure that sobered them all considerably. An officer escorted them to one of the parking levels and left them to search through a sea of impounded cars.

After a few moments of aimless wandering Howie suddenly threw his head back in glee and emitted the group yell. The six began to run towards the white van, then stopped short and stared. There in the front seat was Artie, wearing a policeman's hat and licking at a chocolate ice cream cone.

Spying them, he waved. "Hi."

Despite the dim light Kevin risked a picture.

Rob rushed forward. "Artie! Why, you—"

A bare-headed policeman appeared. "This your van? I guess that makes you the idiot responsible for losing this cute little kid. Now listen, buster. This is a big city, and if you can't look after kids you've got no business being a counselor."

"But officer—"

"And while you're at it you might watch where you park your van. This is going to cost you sixty-five bucks. Stop by the cashier on your way out. Now beat it." He turned to Artie. "So long, kid. Take care of yourself." He put his hat back on his head, tossed a contemptuous look at Rob and walked out of view.

Opting for self control, Rob took a deep breath. "All right, let's get out of here."

A piece of America

The white van, now a bit gray after its trials and tribulations in the soot of New York, finally drove through the gate of the Long Island campground at seven-thirty that night. Tired and hungry, the eight occupants piled out to find Charlie Butcher waiting for them, his face an unhealthy shade of purple.

"Are you Nevin and Leaver from Canada?"

"That's us." Dennis tried to sound cheerful.

"Get over here!" For the benefit of the campers, Butcher forced a smile and added, "We'll just be a few minutes, fellas." He turned to Dennis and Rob with murder in his eye. "You're late, and you know how I feel about that. And that van looks disgusting! Everyone else is going to the drive-in tonight but you don't get to go. Feed those kids and wash the van. And don't let me catch you being late again." He hopped into a dark sedan and sped off.

"Who does he think he is?" complained Dennis. "He could at least have let us explain ... "

Rob groaned. "If we explained what happened

35

today he'd probably fire us on the spot. Just be grateful he didn't find out."

So it was that when the bulk of the Juniortours contingent returned from their showing of *The Cheese People* later that night, they found the campers and counselors of the Ambulance up to their ears in suds, scrubbing their van.

"Hey, Ambulance," heckled one of the Road Hogs counselors as he drove by. "What are you doing— sterilizing?"

Dennis flushed red. "This is mortifying!"

Rob grabbed a polishing cloth. "If you had any sense, Dennis, you'd worry less about your public image and more about the little Houdini we have to cart around. He's real trouble, and I have a feeling this is only the tip of the iceberg."

Sheldon's voice wafted over from the other side of the van, where he was polishing the hubcaps. "This reminds me of the time Pete Ogrodnick and I had a big car wash for charity ... "

"Artie'll be okay," said Dennis abstractedly.

"You're missing the point," Rob insisted. "I'm not even worried about him disappearing so much as where he's going. What does he *do* with those hours on his own? Today I asked him where he went and he said, 'Oh, no place.'"

"Theirs isn't much better," said Dennis.

"What?"

"Their name. Road Hogs. Road *Hogs*. Great name for a bunch of pigs."

"Dennis, pay attention! We're sitting on a time-bomb here!"

"I knew those guys were going to be trouble as

soon as they moved in on our women," Dennis mused.

"Wipe that look off your face!" Rob commanded. "We've got problems! This is no time to start a gang war!"

"Road Hogs!"

"All right, Dennis, you've called all the shots up to now. It's my turn. We're going to forget about the Road Hogs, we're going to accept the fact that we're the Ambulance and we're going to spend the rest of the trip watching Artie like hawks. I don't care if we don't get a date between here and California. He's not getting away again!"

* * *

The next day the counselors and campers of Ambulance group headed for the Hayden Planetarium of the New York Museum of Natural History for that morning's showing of "The Stars and Beyond."

From the instant the group left the van Artie Geller found himself under heavy guard. Dennis and Rob walked closely on either side of him, matching his pace exactly, discouraging any attempt to wander ahead or lag behind. The group gained admission to the museum with their Juniortours pass and began to view the exhibits.

Howie, it turned out, had been a closet astronomer since age six, and his bubbling enthusiasm and technical explanations quickly got on everyone's nerves. Not since the introduction of Pete Ogrodnick had the group been so bored by one of its members. It was with relief that they seated themselves in the domed theater, the two counselors carefully flanking Artie.

The theater darkened. The show was an interesting discussion of astronomy, enhanced by a spectacular projector display on the domed ceiling. Twice an usherette had to restrain Howie from taking an active part, but gradually everyone settled down to enjoy the performance.

Finally the soothing music swelled to an exciting crescendo as the film recreated the birth of the universe, and the lights came on to reveal Dennis and Rob, separated by an empty seat.

Coincidentally, attack jelly went on sale in the Wall Street financial district. It was enjoying enormous popularity and sales were heavy. When his stock was sold out Artie stopped at one of the many nearby banks to convert his gains into bigger bills, since storage space in the attaché case was limited. He also dropped by his suppliers' establishments where, as an affluent cash customer, he was greeted warmly. Tomorrow was to be his last day in New York, and Artie arranged to have an enormous farewell supply of attack jelly shipped to Brooklyn's Coney Island, where the tour planned to proceed, weather permitting. Finally, after dodging into a restaurant washroom where he changed out of his tuxedo, he hailed a cab and rushed uptown in time to meet the Ambulance and its frantic counselors for the planned picnic lunch at Central Park Zoo.

When Artie disappeared at Coney Island the next day Rob was more aggravated than surprised. Why was it that an eleven-year-old kid could slip out from under his gaze so effortlessly? He was watching, really he was. He had sent six kids onto the roller coaster, and five had emerged.

"Where's Artie?" Rob asked, eyes wild.

"He left again," said Nick in disgust. "I guess he's going to be doing this from now on. Hey, let's go on the parachute jump!"

"Yeah! With Dennis!" cheered Howie.

"Well, I don't know if Dennis will want to go this time," said Rob. "He got pretty sick last drop."

Dennis walked over, a little pasty-faced but smiling. "Hi, guys. How was the roller coaster?"

"Why don't you ask a more pertinent question," said Rob darkly, "like 'Where's Artie?'"

At that moment Artie was opening the lockers where his supplies were stored. From storage he proceeded to a change room, where assembly took place, and then to a heavily traveled spot on the boardwalk. Attack jelly sales began in earnest. If the sophisticated New Yorker had been delighted by Artie's product and pitch, the tourist found the ten-dollar investment too good to be true. One visitor from Montreal commented to his family that attack jelly and its tuxedo-clad vendor were "a true sampling of New York atmosphere."

Business boomed for much of the afternoon. When his stock was sold out Artie returned to the change room, stashed earnings and tuxedo in his briefcase and went to look for Ambulance group.

By this time Dennis had decided to start working on the tan he intended to perfect during the summer. Greased like a griddle he lay on the beach looking like something that had washed in with the tide. The campers were in the ocean, jumping the breakers and experimenting with the group yell under water. Rob was watching them and at the same time keeping an eye open for Artie. He noticed that several other Juniortours groups were around, both at the beach and in the amusement area. And he couldn't help casting an occasional glance at the various female counselors, lounging in bathing suits or digging in the sand with their charges. The Road Hogs, of course, were nearest the greatest concentration of girls. Allowing their campers to do whatever they pleased, the two counselors were indulging in a boisterous game of frisbee with much shouting and flexing of muscles. A wayward throw caused the larger of the two to tear headlong across the sand in order to make the spectacular catch.

"*Oof!*"

A big foot pounded heavily on Dennis's stomach, jack-knifing his arms and legs into the air as the Road Hogs counselor deftly caught the frisbee with his index finger. Wielding his catch, he turned.

"Hey, sorry about that, pal. I was just..." He looked down at Dennis and a wide grin of recognition spread across his face. "Hey, call an *ambulance!*" He jogged off laughing loudly. An answering chorus of guffaws was heard from the Juniortours people.

Rob rushed over. "Are you all right?"

"Just a little winded!" gasped Dennis in agony.

Rob looked with disgust at the resumed frisbee tournament. "What idiots! We're going to have to stay out of their way."

Dennis rubbed his stomach gingerly. "We're definitely going to have to do something about them. Why not right now?"

"I've got four reasons why not right now," said Rob. "First, this beach is policed by people who probably don't think too much of brawls; second, with Artie missing we can't afford to get thrown out of Coney Island; third, you're in a weakened condition from being sick on all those rides and getting stomped on; and fourth, those gorillas outweigh us by about a hundred pounds, and I don't want my face converted into hamburger. How's that for reasons?"

Dennis breathed deeply. "Well, anyway, here comes Artie."

Rob's eyes followed his partner's. Along the beach, his bare feet splashing in the surf, marched Artie Geller, dressed only in a bathing suit. Around his neck hung the leather pouch and in his hand he carried the inevitable attaché case.

"This time we should really nail him!" Rob seethed. "We should get on his back and not lay off until he tells us where he's been going for the past four days!"

"Aw, come on, Rob," said Dennis, abandoning himself again to the rays of the sun. "This is supposed to be a fun trip. Tomorrow morning we leave for Washington, and I'm sure Artie'll settle down. It's just that New York has an effect on some people, and I guess he's one of them."

"Hi, Rob, Dennis." Artie sat down on the blanket and gazed out to sea, hugging his case on his lap. "Nice day, isn't it?"

"Where have you been?" stormed Rob. He knew the answer would make him no wiser, but his system needed the outlet.

"Oh—nowhere much."

"What have you been up to?"

"Nothing special."

"Then why can't you do it with us?"

"I don't know." Artie waved amiably at his fellow campers in the surf.

* * *

There were no activities planned for the Juniortours people that night, since the groups were packing in preparation for moving on the next morning. A few radios were playing, and some of the campers were running around in a pick-up game of tag, but apart from that the camp was relatively quiet.

"Smile, Dennis." From his crouch just inside the tent flap Kevin snapped a picture, then picked up a stenographer's notebook and wrote, *Roll 2, exposure 8. Dennis smearing cream on bad sunburn.* He chewed his pencil thoughtfully and added, *Note redness of shoulders and nose.*

Dennis was disgusted. "Aw, Kevin, this isn't the kind of stuff you want to capture on film. Surely there are better things to remember about this trip than my suffering."

"The way things have been going, I'd say it's one of the high points," said Rob sourly. "Put me down for a print of that one."

Nick, Howie, Sam and Sheldon marched into the

tent and sat down in varying attitudes of discontent.

"Hey, guys, what happened to the tag game?" asked Dennis, slipping into a T-shirt as carefully as possible.

Sam snorted. "It's all politics. I was *it;* some guy came too close and I tagged him. He said I didn't touch him, and since I don't have as many connections as he does everybody listened to him. So I tagged him again—my fist, his face—and the game broke up."

"Aw, Sam," Rob groaned, "we're supposed to get along with everybody."

Sam shrugged. "Who wants to get along with a guy who won't admit when he's tagged?"

Nick, Howie, Kevin and Sheldon nodded in agreement.

Rob sighed heavily. "All right, everybody. Let's go to sleep."

"Can I stay up a little later?" Sheldon requested. "I want to finish my letter to Pete."

"Well, okay, but make it fast." Artie had taken one hundred percent of Rob's energy, leaving him powerless to cope with anything else. All evening he had tried to worm out of Artie the details—any details—of his activities on his solitary excursions. It was like talking to a loaf of bread. Steady grilling, wheedling, shaming and threatening served only to turn up the information that Artie had been "no place," where he had done "nothing much," after which he had come back to the group. The kid was a clam and, most perplexing of all, had spent the rest of the evening reading his tour book, a thick volume entitled *Take a Piece of America Home With You*. Suddenly he was the greatest tourist in the world.

As the group bedded down Rob found himself sleepless despite his exhaustion. After struggling into his jeans he crawled out of the tent to join Dennis, who had been unable to go to bed upon discovering that the sunburn cream had epoxied his shirt to his blistered shoulders. The medicinal smell of the cream hung heavy in the air, and it was this that brought Cindy and Vera, the counselors of the Bluebirds, over to the Ambulance.

Rising above his pain, Dennis became suddenly sociable. Although the girls were only interested in borrowing some burn cream, he was greatly encouraged.

"Cindy and Vera," he sighed, a goofy grin replacing his painful grimace.

Rob laughed. "Earth calling Dennis. Face it: they only love us for our burn cream."

"Ah, but my instincts, Nevin. My instincts say this is the start of a beautiful relationship."

"Your instincts also told you you were getting a tan."

"Cool it, Nevin."

A day at the races

Roll 3, exposure 2. Rob following Artie around in Washington. Note Dennis at souvenir shop.

The Ambulance made Washington just after noon and began to tour the city as per instructions. They drove around in the van, stopping at various monuments and historic sites. They took the White House tour and improvised their own tour of the Capitol Hill area, including a peek at the chambers of the Senate and the House of Representatives.

Throughout all this Rob kept a sharp eye on Artie, who made absolutely no attempt to lag behind or run ahead, and who was looking around with great interest. Rob allowed himself a little cautious optimism. Perhaps Dennis was right and the New York episode was a one-of-a-kind thing. Still, one couldn't be too careful.

Dennis, of course, reached his glory at the souvenir shops. The dome of the Capitol building gleamed from his head, and he was festooned with flags and bunting.

45

Kevin was driving everyone crazy with his fine eye for photographic composition. It was nothing to him that the group had to stand around posing for half an hour at a time, waiting for the sun to come out from behind a cloud. Ultimately Sam had to speed up this process with friendly threats of violence. Sheldon, of course, kept the conversation lively with endless tidbits of useless information, most of them about Pete Ogrodnick. Much to everyone's annoyance, Howie caught sight of a poster advertising the Air and Space Museum at the Smithsonian Institution, and began to nag vigorously to be taken there at once. An on-the-spot referendum was held and Ambulance group voted unanimously to visit the Smithsonian to shut Howie up.

When they finally pulled into the campsite at half past seven, they were all exhausted and glowing from the first day yet that had gone without mishap. Rob was almost happy, especially when he caught a sideways wink from Dennis as the Ambulance pulled into the spot directly adjacent to the van marked *Bluebirds*.

"We can't park here," announced Nick solemnly.

Rob turned. "Why not?"

"It's space 14," Nick explained.

"So?"

"The unlucky number. If we park here we'll have bad luck."

Dennis chuckled. "You mean 13. The unlucky number is 13. And there is no 13 in this camp."

Nick pointed to the space which held the Bluebirds' van. "That's 12, and we're in the space right next to it. People think they can avoid the unlucky number by leaving it out, but that just makes 14 the *real* unlucky number. We'd better not park here."

"Now look, Nick," began Rob, who had caught sight of Vera in the van's side mirror. "This is all superstition."

"Once when my Dad went bowling he got lane 14 and in the middle of the game he dropped the ball on his big toe, and the swelling didn't go down for a year and a half. And once in Toronto we had this hotel room on the fourteenth floor, and wouldn't you know it, the toilet backed up. And once—"

"But, Nick," Dennis reasoned, "we're all tired and this is a good spot near the washrooms. We don't really have the strength to look for another one."

"What about 15?" Nick suggested.

"Forget it," said Rob. "We're staying here."

"Well, okay, Rob, but when terrible things start to happen don't say I didn't warn you."

* * *

Throwing his arms upward, Dennis yawned at the night sky. "Ah, Nevin, this is the way life was meant to be."

Rob leaned back against the door of the van and rested his arm on the outside mirror. "It looks like things are taking a turn for the better," he admitted.

Dennis sighed. "A starry sky, Washington, D.C., and most important, a rendezvous with two charming young Bluebirds tomorrow night. What better has life to offer, Nevin?"

"Good old lucky 14."

"We'd better hit the sack. We've got a big day tomorrow, and an even bigger evening."

"By the way," asked Rob, "where are we taking the ladies?"

"Don't worry about that now. Women admire spontaneity. When the moment is upon us we'll make our decision."

The two entered the tent, undressed and climbed into their bedrolls. Dennis was soon snoring lightly.

Rob lay in a sleepy haze, his mind wandering over the events of the past day. In just twenty-four hours his mood had changed from black misery to happiness, contentment and anticipation. Then again, that was to be expected. He'd had a nice day in Washington, Artie hadn't disappeared, and best of all he had a date with Cindy. Or Vera. Dennis— dumb old Dennis—had been right about this trip after all. Even the kids were beginning to grow on him. They were downright nice—Sam with his sublime self-confidence, Howie and his space obsession, Kevin and his camera, Nick and his silly superstition, Sheldon and his motorized mouth. Even Artie was a nice, quiet little guy. And to watch Dennis buy souvenirs—it was all going to be better from here on in.

On that note he drifted off to sleep.

* * *

The next day was hot and sunny, and after breakfast Dennis handed out pens and paper to his six

48

charges. "All right, guys, you've sent your folks a little postcard, but now it's time you wrote them a proper letter. Go to it."

Sam moaned. "Aw, come on. I don't want to write a letter. I'll tell them all about it when I get home."

"Write," ordered Rob.

The six boys deployed themselves about the area. Sheldon, Howie and Kevin remained at the picnic table where the group had eaten breakfast, Nick and Sam lay on their stomachs on the grass, and Artie propped himself up against a shady tree and used his knee as a writing desk. With his briefcase out of sight on the other side of him, he looked the quintessential boy in his natural habitat—cute, harmless, healthy and intent only on his letter—a picture straight out of a brochure of any summer camp. Even Rob had to smile.

Then he was distracted by Howie's voice. "Hey, guys, we can write all about how the Ambulance got towed away in New York!"

"Yeah!" exclaimed Sam. "Hey, Dennis, how do you spell 'impounded'?"

"Don't write that stuff!" exclaimed Dennis. "Just write, *Having a wonderful time. Love, Whoever.*"

"But you said you wanted a proper letter."

"Well," Dennis explained, "there are certain things we share as a group that we really should keep to ourselves."

"You mean like all that stuff about the police?"

"Yeah."

Rob laughed. "That was a close one, wasn't it?"

Dennis smiled too. "Hurry up, everybody. Washington is waiting for us. Hey, where's Artie?"

All seven pairs of eyes flew to the tree. There sat the pen and paper, and no Artie. Rob darted over and picked up the letter. It read, *Dear Mom and Dad,* and there it ended.

"He was in front of my eyes!" cried Rob, looking around in all directions. "I swear! In front of my eyes!"

"All right," announced Dennis in what was becoming a regular speech. "Everybody stay calm. Don't panic."

Rob's eyes darted about the camp. "He's disappeared!"

Letters forgotten, the seven ran out to the highway and anxiously scanned the area in all directions.

Sam frowned. "He's kind of a drag, isn't he? I mean, aren't we good enough for him?"

"Why did he come on the tour in the first place?" asked Howie in annoyance.

Rob, who had been asking the same question concerning himself, slumped against a telephone pole. "Why me? Why?"

Nick had an answer. "This is all because we parked in space 14. I told you it was just asking for trouble."

Dennis breathed deeply. "Let's just finish the letters and go into town like we planned. Either we'll run into him or he'll find us, like in New York."

"As though things went so well in New York," said Rob sarcastically.

"Cool it, Nevin. Things only go wrong when we lose our heads. Everything's going to be okay."

* * *

On the stroke of nine, Artie Geller, clad in tuxedo and gloves, entered a smart hobby shop in the heart of Washington. He toured the store silently for a few minutes, then borrowed a pen and paper from the manager and began to make a list of his requirements.

The manager's eyes opened wider. "That's going to run into a few bucks, son. Are you sure you can afford it?"

Artie nodded confidently. He slid the paper across the glass counter until it came to rest in front of the man. "I'll have this please, sir. How much?"

Shaking his head, the man rang up the figures on the cash register. "With tax, $579.63." He laughed. "I'll tell you what, kid. You've got five hundred dollars, it's yours."

Casually Artie undid the third button of his ruffled shirt, reached into the leather pouch and came out with a small gold key. This he inserted into the lock of his attaché case. There was a soft click. He lifted the lid to reveal his cash resources. In neat stacks held in place by metal money-clips lay the bills, arranged by denomination. He removed five crisp, new hundreds and placed them on the counter.

The manager made no move to take them. He stood stiff as a statue, staring at the attaché case as Artie closed and locked it, returned the gold key to its pouch and redid his shirt button.

"Do we have a deal?" asked Artie softly.

The man snapped out of his reverie. "Huh? Oh, yeah. Sure." He looked thoughtful as he rang up the sale. "I'll need your help to get all the stuff together. Then maybe I'll close up for the day. Hmmm. And maybe tomorrow I'll fly to Florida. I feel old."

In half an hour Artie was moving through the bustle of Washington's morning traffic, towing a wagon laden with packages, boxes and bags. The load teetered dangerously as he pulled it up Capitol Hill to a spot on the grassy parkland overlooked by the Capitol building. It was level and offered two major benefits—it was heavily traveled, and it was virtually out of sight of the security sentries because of the slope of the land.

Setting to work, Artie removed the strings from his parcels and began to unpack. He opened the auto-racing set first, and began laying eight lanes of track in different directions. Then he took out the electric train set and wove its track in and around the road-racing complex. The sight of a boy in a tuxedo crawling on the grass and setting up toys attracted attention, and comments began circulating among the passersby.

In an amazingly short time a staggering system of mechanical toys began to rise from the lawn. A crowd began to gather, and by the time Artie put the last tunnel in place at least fifty people stood watching in fascination.

The set-up was like a miniature city, with systems of track towering in the air, then spiraling back down towards the ground, all supported by tiny metal girders. There were bridges and tunnels, treacherous curves and long straightaways. An elaborate canal system snaked through the complex, patrolled by a small fleet of boats. From the eight-car starting gate, tracks rose to great heights and plunged back to the ground, twisting in loop-the-loops and stretching through giant moving barriers, railroad crossings and jumps over the canal. The tracks crossed and recrossed each other, ultimately merging into one single lane just before the finishing gate. Leading from the whole arrangement was an intricate system of wires attached to huge battery packs.

Awestruck, the crowd stared at the wonder that lay glinting in the bright sunlight before them.

"It's beautiful!" declared one woman.

"Son," said a man, "when I was your age I had a pretty nice model train set, but now I'm not ashamed to admit that you just rewrote the book with this set-up. Would you mind telling us what it is?"

From a box Artie carefully removed eight cars, identical but for color, and placed them in the starting gate, which also served as the energy charger. "This is just a trial run, of course," he said to the crowd. "Which car do you think will win?"

Immediately intrigued, the spectators stared even harder, attempting to untangle the spaghetti-like jumble of track that each car would travel. It was a hopeless task.

"Let 'er rip, kid!"

Artie energized the cars and released the starting

gate. Eight streaks of color launched off in different directions. Blue and white shot forward, then diverged into a V. Red flew through a dazzling loop-the-loop. Green and yellow shot down steep hills and hurtled across the canal. Orange screamed around a sharp curve and shot through a tunnel. Black and purple took off, seemingly in the wrong direction, then zoomed through a number of manoeuvers and hurtled for the finish line. There was a murmur of delight and scattered applause from the crowd as the eight cars converged on the final single stretch. With four lanes left, blue pulled ahead of orange, green ahead of red, yellow ahead of purple and black ahead of white. The next fork in the road left blue and green in the lead, barreling towards the single lane and victory. Green squeaked through the gate first, amid wild applause from the growing crowd.

Artie arranged the eight cars back in the starting gate and waited for the ovation to die down before making his pitch. "Would anyone care to make this a little more interesting? I pay three-to-one for the winner."

A roar of appreciation erupted from the crowd and money began to appear in eager hands.

"Before I take your stakes I feel it's only fair to tell you that under the actual race conditions there are other factors involved than what you've just seen. Not all cars finish the race. You see—"

"We saw the game, kid," said a man Artie recognized as a senior United States Senator. "Let's get on with it. Can you take a bet as large as five dollars on that green car?"

"Certainly, sir," said Artie. "Just let me organize the table." On the empty wagon he arranged eight small trays, each one corresponding to the color of a car. He rolled the wagon close to the crowd, looked up and smiled engagingly. *"Faites vos jeux.* No limits on betting—and no coins, please."

Money appeared from everywhere. Heavy betting went on the green car, but a considerable sum went down on second-place blue, and the occasional bet went on the other six cars. When Artie withdrew the wagon the biggest bet was the Senator's five-dollar bill.

"We'll just take the kid for a few bucks and leave him alone," the Senator chuckled to his aides. "You know—just to teach him a lesson."

Artie walked over to the power pack and flicked the switch. The miniature city came alive. Two electric trains began moving along separate tracks and boats began to sail through the canal. The blades of three enormous windmill tunnels started rotating slowly, and at four points along the track mechanical moose crossed back and forth. Most hazardous of all, six pile-drivers suspended by wires above the arrangement worked relentlessly, pounding at the track.

The crowd stared, dumbfounded.

Artie energized the cars and released them again.

The race began much as before, except that this time the crowd, now almost a hundred strong, was cheering wildly. The first disaster came when yellow, fresh out of the starting gate, went into the jump for the canal and rammed head-on into the smokestack of a passing luxury liner. The car flew through the air and hit the grass, tires still spinning. This demonstration of sudden death heightened the spectators' excitement as they followed their own cars and cheered vigorously. A woman screamed as the blade of a windmill swept purple off the track. Orange disappeared from sight in a tunnel and came into view again for only a fraction of a second before being caught right over the front wheels by a pile-drive. It flipped gracelessly through the air and came to rest in the coal car of one of the trains, which was itself continuing towards a railroad crossing. The red car was approaching the same crossing.

"Faster, red! Faster, red! *Faster!*" A man covered his eyes as the train hit red broadside, sending it careering off the roadway.

The Senator was jumping up and down, screaming himself hoarse. As he had logically reasoned, green was the best car. It was hurtling along well ahead of the pack towards the single lane and an easy victory. That fifteen dollars was as good as his.

Crash! Before the horrified eyes of most of the bettors, a moose stepped out onto the track and wiped out the much-favored green. A great sigh arose.

The smart money was still on blue, which was speeding towards the single track. The black car was also headed for the single track, but from the other side. All eyes were on that intersection as the two cars hit the merging point at the same moment, kissed briefly, then flew off the track in opposite directions. The shocked spectators stared as white, the only car left, glided steadily to the finish line, the victor.

56

"Oh, yeah!" From the depths of the crowd danced a joyful Congressman, punching at the air and chanting, "White! White! White!" as he ran up to collect his payoff, three dollars. He nudged the Senator. "I was the only one with the faith to bet on white! What foresight!"

As their emotions slowly calmed, the spectators watched while Artie dumped the rest of the money—his winnings—into the large carton that had held the train set, and placed the cars again.

* * *

Dennis sorted through a stack of bald eagle T-shirts, selected one and held it to his body. "How about this? Good? Or maybe too much red, white and blue?"

"Buy it," said Rob in agitation. "You already own everything else."

"Come on, Rob. Loosen up. We're sightseeing."

"May I remind you that one of the sights we're supposed to see is Artie? He's not here, so let's move on."

"Amen to that," said Sam. "You've seen one monument, you've seen them all."

"Hey, look at this!" exclaimed Dennis. "House of Representatives steak knives. Maybe a present for my folks."

"Dennis—"

"Why don't we hit the Smithsonian Air and Space Museum again?" suggested Howie.

"Forget it," said everybody.

"I'm hungry," announced Sheldon, not for the

first time. "Maybe Artie's hungry too and we'll catch him at the restaurant."

Rob threw up his hands in surrender. "Okay, it's almost lunch time anyway. Let's eat."

* * *

Roll 3, exposure 35. Dennis eating enchillada.

"Red is the winner," announced Artie over the tumultuous cheering of the crowd. "The house is now paying off for red."

"I must have the worst luck in the world," complained the Senator sullenly. "Any car I bet on— *bang!* It hits a moose. Why always a moose? I'd almost welcome a train or a boat."

"Trying again, Senator?" inquired Artie as people crowded around the wagon to place their bets.

"Yeah. I'll put ten bucks on white. Who ever heard of a road race with a moose in it anyway?"

In that particular race green was the winner, while the hapless white met with a moose fairly early on.

In little more than an hour interest in Artie's road-racing casino had reached a dizzying peak. The crowd was never less than two hundred strong as departing spectators were replaced by fresh passersby with fresh money. Senators and Congressmen, civil servants high and low, diplomats foreign and domestic, and tourists from all over the world converged on one spot on Capitol Hill. Some stayed for a few minutes, some longer. Most left a little bit poorer, but all took with them the feeling that they

58

had participated in something wonderful.

But the real die-hard was the Senator, still await-
ing his first triumph of the day as Artie announced
the final race.

"All right, kid, you've busted me." He turned his
empty pockets inside-out to illustrate his point.
"See? All I've got left is four bucks, and I'm going to
put it on the green car. Kid, if there's any justice, I
need a win, because if I lose I'm going to have to hit
my secretary up for cab fare home!"

Artie smiled slightly and rolled out the betting
table. Eager hands pushed money at it. The Senator
laid down his final stakes and all the others, knowing him to be a notorious loser, cast their cash elsewhere. Bettors racked their brains for the inspira-
tion to make that last bet count. When Artie re-
trieved the betting wagon the amount of money
placed there easily tripled anything that had been
wagered so far. The Senator stood at the front of
the crowd, staring at the starting gate with intense
concentration.

The green car was in trouble immediately. A pile-
driver caught it on the rear bumper, holding it in
place, front wheels in the air, back wheels spinning
out the electric charge to no avail. The other seven
cars continued their mad pace along the track.

A distinguished looking businessman threw his
custom-tailored jacket to the grass and began
stomping on it in a fury of frustration as the yellow
car struck a three-masted schooner and bounced out
of play. A Senate page swallowed his gum as white
met its end on the turn of a windmill blade. Two
diplomats who had heavy stakes on black broke into

excited Cantonese as their car headed for the finish line. In unison, both uttered an untranslatable monosyllable as their hopes were pile-driven mere inches from the home stretch. Red, purple, blue and orange were still in play. Everyone watched excitedly. It was going to be close. Green was still pinned down, wheels spinning. The four live cars shot through the hazards, missing them all, and rocketed towards the lane merge. It looked as though a crash was inevitable.

Miraculously the field survived and sped neck-and-neck to the next merge. By a hair, orange pulled in ahead of blue, and red led purple by a bumper. As the cars headed for the final merge and what looked like a photo finish, red and purple touched wheels. That was all it took. For an instant the cars were arranged in a tight rectangle. Then they were sailing through the air, north, south, east and west. The crowd gasped. There would be no winner.

But suddenly the spinning wheels of the green car stopped and the front end fell back to the roadway, jarring the car loose from the pile-driver's grasp. Propelled almost entirely by the force of gravity, green rolled slowly down the track. It moved through the windmill tunnel, across two sets of train tracks and past another pile-driver. Now the crowd had fallen dead silent, holding its breath. The Senator was on his hands and knees by the track in a desperate bid to will the car over the finish line. A moose appeared and green moved into it with a gentle *clink*. When it withdrew, the car was still on the track, inching towards glory.

"He did it!" gasped the Senator. "He beat the moose! Come on, green, come on! Please!"

Still moving at a snail's pace, green entered the four-lane merge, then the two, and headed down the home stretch, urged on by the Senator's demented yelling. It rolled down the road right up to the finish line—and stopped dead.

The Senator wailed in agony. All at once the spectators broke into hysterical laughter. Artie looked at the betting wagon. The Senator's last four dollars stood alone on the green tray, dwarfed by the mounds of money piled on the others. Artie reached out his foot and nudged the green car over the line.

The Senator was almost in tears.

Cost-cutting

By mid-afternoon the white van was on the highway again, heading for the campsite. Dennis was at the wheel, quietly serene, while Rob simmered like a boiling saucepan, its contents threatening to spill over.

"If he's not there," he promised, "I'll kill myself!"

"Take it easy, Nevin," soothed Dennis. "Of course he's there. Where else would he be?"

"Where? Anywhere! We don't know where he goes when he disappears! He could be in orbit by now!"

"Stop yelling. You'll upset the guys. Now, look. We'll be in camp in five minutes, and Artie'll be there waiting for us. Once we get dinner out of the way we're laughing. Come eight o'clock, off we waltz with our companions for the evening, the Beauteous Bluebirds. Look on the bright side."

"But Dennis, there *is* no bright side! We've lost a kid!"

"He isn't lost," Dennis insisted. "Yes, okay, so he isn't with us. But that doesn't mean he's lost."

"It doesn't?" piped Sheldon from the back seat.

"No, it doesn't," said Dennis. "It means he's away —for a little while."

"I don't buy that," said Sam. "When I was seven I had a gerbil, Igor. My parents told me Igor went away for a while. Turns out he's dead! What a snow job!"

"Artie isn't dead!" cried Rob in agitation. "He's just—away for a while!"

"Now look what you've done," whispered Dennis. "You've upset the kids. Just take it easy. I've got everything worked out. Starting tomorrow we make a conscious effort to pull together as a group. We can get Artie so involved in the activities that he won't want to go off on his own anymore. And we'll be the best darn van on the whole tour. But tonight we take off our counselors' hats and slip into our dancing shoes. If we play our cards right, Rob, we could be seeing these girls all summer." The van turned into the campground and headed for spot 14. "See? What did I tell you? There's Artie. Hmmm. Who's that with him?"

"It's Mr. Butcher," said Howie. "I guess you and Rob are going to get chewed out now."

Butcher and Artie were seated on the ground in spot 14. They got up and moved over to lean on the Bluebirds' vehicle, allowing Dennis to park.

Butcher's face was suffused with anger as he turned murderous eyes on Dennis and Rob.

"Where in blazes have you been? I've been here with your camper for more than an hour!"

"We have a lost—that is, we were looking for—" Rob stammered.

"He wasn't lost!" raged Butcher. "*You* were lost!"

"Well," Dennis began, "ha, ha, I guess it was all a misunderstanding. And everything's all cleared up now. We're here, see?"

"You Canadian Ambulance guys are more trouble than you're worth!" howled Butcher as a crowd of curious spectators began to gather. "These parents are spending money so their kids can see the country and have a good time! And *your* group is always in a shambles!"

"We're having a good time!" said Sam belligerently, jumping to the defense of his counselors. "We're having just as much fun as any other group."

"More, even," said Howie, "because we've got the Ambulance."

"And I'm getting some great shots," added Kevin, patting his film canister.

Butcher forced a benign smile. "I'm glad you boys are—uh—enjoying yourselves. But this is really between your counselors and me."

The five boys disappeared into the van. Artie followed.

Butcher was grateful that the group was having fun. That gave him slight grounds for not firing Dennis and Rob. If he fired them it would be a big pain in the neck and would mean lots of paperwork. And he'd have to replace them. If he couldn't he'd have to take over the group himself—the thought made him cringe. Long distance driving—*with kids!*

By now several of the groups were watching with

interest and enjoyment as Butcher tore a strip off Dennis and Rob. Rob could see Cindy and Vera on the sidelines.

"Anyway," Butcher raged, "if even one of your campers gets lost again, that's it. And as for that kid Artie, obviously he wanders. Keep an eye on him, you idiots! Are you listening?"

Dennis nodded. "Yes, sir." He refrained from pointing out that the whole camp was listening.

"Now here's the reason I wanted to talk to you in the first place, before you went and got yourselves lost! Head office just got charged forty bucks for your speeding ticket on the New York Thruway. We don't pay for your heavy foot! I want that money right now!"

Dennis scrambled into the van and opened the cash box.

"Mr. Butcher, could we have a word with you?" Rob began.

"No!" he bawled. "Haven't you wasted enough of my time already? I'm a busy man. I don't like spending hours sitting in a trailer camp!" Dennis emerged with the money and Butcher snapped it out of his hands. "Now, I don't want to hear from you Canadian Ambulance guys again. If you want to keep your jobs, make sure the rest of this trip is perfect!" He stormed off.

Since Dennis's and Rob's humiliating dressing-down was over, the crowd of counselors and campers began to disperse. Cindy and Vera approached, all sympathy.

"Gee, guys, that was terrible," said Cindy. "I felt so sorry for you."

"Pay no attention to Butcher," said Dennis with a dazzling smile. "He gets very emotional at times. It didn't bother us a bit, did it, Rob?"

"Not a bit," Rob barely whispered, his face gray.

"Anyway," Dennis went on, "we'll feed our kids and get everybody all settled in, and we'll be by to pick you up at eight."

"Oh, we just couldn't," said Vera.

Dennis looked stricken. "Pardon?"

"Well, it's obvious you have an internal problem in your group. You have to stay with the boys tonight and work it out."

"No we don't!" blurted Dennis. "That is, I think it can wait till tomorrow—"

"We just wouldn't feel right taking your time away from your jobs."

"But our kids are fine!" Dennis insisted. "Aren't they, Rob?"

"Peachy."

"See? And we promised you girls a good time tonight."

"Oh, don't you worry about us," said Vera. "We'll find something to do. Byron and Darryl are going to a movie and they said we could go along with them."

"Byron and Darryl?" asked Dennis weakly.

"Oh, don't you know them? The Road Hogs."

"I didn't know their names," muttered Dennis through clenched teeth.

"Well, anyway," said Vera, "I think it's better this way. Your kids need you. But thanks for the invitation." The girls rejoined their own campers.

Dennis cast a wounded look at Rob. "Well,

Nevin, it's in the toilet. Thanks a lot."

"Me? Why me? If you're going to be mad at someone, try Artie!"

Shaking his head, Dennis stepped into the van. "You *stunk* out there, Nevin. You added nothing to the conversation."

"There was nothing to add! The afternoon was a disaster, so I don't see any reason why the evening should be any different! Now, while we're still good and mad let's do a number on Artie!"

"We can't do a number on Artie," said Dennis. "If we're going to understand him we have to analyse his personality traits."

"I have a better idea," said Rob grimly. "You hold him and I'll hit him. Then we'll switch. How's that for analysis?"

"Rob!" Dennis was horrified. "He's only a little kid!"

"Oh? Of course you remember that these kids are men. So Artie is a man. Yes, a very *sick* man."

"Look," said Dennis, "I don't see why you should blame Artie because you have no finesse with women. I hope the Road Hogs are properly grateful to you for handing them our dates on a silver platter!"

The group began to set up the tent. It was as they were preparing dinner that Rob finally blew up. "All right, Artie, where were you?"

"Nowhere."

"Don't give me that! Everybody is somewhere! I want to know where *you* were!"

"Nowhere much."

"What were you doing?"

"Nothing."

"Then why did it take you all day?"

"Traffic."

"Traffic? From breakfast till afternoon, traffic? Listen, you—"

Dennis took over. "You know, Artie, don't get me wrong. We respect your individuality, but we can't help being a little hurt when you hardly spend any time with us. So now you've had your little side trips and we can enjoy the rest of the tour as a group. Okay?"

Artie nodded vaguely.

Dennis leaned over to Rob. "You see, Nevin, this is how you deal with kids. Speak reasonably and show understanding, and everything's cool."

"I congratulate you on your sensitivity," said Rob acidly. "But until I know where he's been going all this time, I don't intend to be reasonable about anything."

Dennis snorted. "You're such a pessimist. If Artie disappears again I will be very surprised."

Rob's face twisted. "Your surprise will be a great comfort to me."

"What are we going to do tonight?" asked Howie, reaching for a hot dog.

"Nothing," snapped Rob. "We're going to stay here and lick our wounds and pray that tomorrow will be a better day."

There was much honking and waving as the Road Hogs drove out of camp, accompanied by the Bluebirds. For Dennis it was the bitterest pill of all.

Roll 4, exposure 15. Dennis looking glum.

68

Roll 4, exposure 16. Rob looking glum.
Roll 4, exposure 17. Dennis and Rob together,
both looking glum.

* * *

Still in disgrace, Ambulance group slunk out of
Washington the next morning, heading west on Interstate 70 towards Pittsburgh.

As Dennis put it, "Nothing wipes out a bad repu-
tation better than distance."

Rob laughed mirthlessly. "What good does that
do? Everyone else is moving with us."

"It doesn't matter," said Dennis confidently.
"Anything that happened in Washington is another
universe when you're in Pittsburgh." He turned to
the boys. "You know, this whole group has been too
down lately. We've got to do something about that."
He then legislated a "good mood" policy. Unhappi-
ness was prohibited. "Come on, guys! We should be
doing things that lift our spirits."

Sheldon nodded approvingly. "That's exactly
what Pete used to say."

"I'm so glad," muttered Rob.

"How about the group yell?" suggested Howie.
"That lifts our spirits."

"Anything but the group yell," Dennis amended.

"You know, I don't want to preach," said Nick,
"but we never would have had any trouble if you'd
listened to me in the first place and moved out of
spot 14. I hope you won't make that mistake again."

"I have an announcement to make," said Rob,
who was driving. "We have a guest. Everybody,

meet Artie. He's going to be touring with us today and from now on without disappearing at all. Isn't that right, Artie?"

Artie looked up from the depths of *Take a Piece of America Home With You*. "Right."

"Hey, that's great, Artie," said Kevin, "because you're in hardly any of my shots."

By noon the group had made Pittsburgh, where they had lunch in a public park and headed for U.S. Steel. Juniortours had arranged for a guided tour of a steel mill and research laboratory. A young engineer led Ambulance and two other groups through the various facilities. Unfortunately one of the other crews was Byron and Darryl and the Road Hogs, who peppered the afternoon with ambulance jokes. In spite of this the campers thoroughly enjoyed the experience, although it was touch and go when Kevin was told he could not bring his camera inside and Sam, taking his part, lectured the bewildered security guard on the true meaning of freedom.

Dennis's mood perked up when the tour reached its end at the U.S. Steel souvenir shop, where he picked up three strings of steel beads, a steel bracelet and a sixteen-pound block of pure steel.

Rob occupied himself with watching Artie, who seemed content to follow the tour. While he appeared interested in the information delivered by the guard, he never asked a question or strayed from his path to see something. Throughout he kept a purely passive expression on his face.

After an early supper the group drove on to Columbus, Ohio, where they were to spend the night.

"Watch where you park," advised Nick as Dennis pulled wearily into the Olentangy Indian Caverns campground.

"Okay, everybody," announced Dennis. "We'll set up the tent, and you guys go right to sleep. We've got a big day ahead of us tomorrow."

* * *

"You know, Rob," said Dennis, sitting on the grass in front of the van after the group was bedded down and quiet. "There's only one problem with this trip."

"Wow," said Rob sarcastically. "I can hardly wait to hear which one of our many disasters has percolated down to you as a full-fledged problem."

"We're seeing so many great places and so many great things that it's getting expensive. My money's running out. Do you know that I'm down to a hundred bucks?"

Rob was appalled. "But I paid all our fines! I got our van out of hock! I've only got two hundred left myself! We can't *afford* to go to California!"

"Where's it all going?" asked Dennis.

Rob snorted in disgust. "Where do you think? On your head, on your back, on your wrist, around your waist—it's that stupid junk you keep buying. Why did you need that lump you bought at the mill today?"

"But, Rob, it's pure steel. I have to have souvenirs of our trip. Anyway, don't worry. We can always dip into the tour money if we run a little

71

short. Then we'll cut a few costs, and no one will know the difference."

"Butcher will know the difference," Rob reminded him grimly. "Probably to the penny. If we go over budget we'll be killed."

"Oh, I'm sure we get a few dollars leeway," said Dennis airily. "Everything'll be great. And now that Artie's giving us no more trouble—"

"I wouldn't exactly put it that way, Dennis. He gave us twenty-four hours of relative peace. That's the best I can say for him. Who knows what tomorrow may bring?"

"Nevin, you can be so shallow sometimes. Can't you see how we're pulling the group together? Pretty soon not only will our guys be taking care of Artie, but they'll also be taking care of each other. And the true brilliance of this plan is that it leaves us free to seek some companionship of the female persuasion."

"You're a dreamer," said Rob sourly. "The fact is, this trip stunk on paper and it stinks in reality. Everyone on the tour heard Butcher rip us up. We're the big Juniortours joke this summer. I don't think you realize exactly how much trouble we're in. We're in the middle of a foreign country with most of our money gone, and one of our kids just does what he pleases whenever he wants to and we can't stop him. I doubt even the great Pete Ogrodnick could figure his way out of this mess."

"That's exactly why we're in such great shape right now," Dennis argued. "I mean, this is rock bottom. It can only get better. We'll have no more problems with Artie, we'll learn to budget, and we'll have a great trip. Soon everyone'll forget about the bad times we had, and the only problem we'll have to deal with is being named the Ambulance, which is a drag, but what can we do?"

Rob looked glum.

Dennis slapped him on the shoulder. "You see that van over there? They call themselves the Rhode Island Reds. They're from Providence. I think one of them winked at me earlier today—either that or she had something in her eye. But I'd say the odds are in our favor. We'll get to know them in the next day or so—you know, just hanging out and letting them see what great guys we are. Then, in Chicago we'll be old friends, and we can take them out."

"What about budgeting?" asked Rob.

"Well, this is a necessity. We can always cut back on—uh—something else. Anyway, I'm tired. Let's go to sleep."

* * *

The brilliance of the morning was dimmed somewhat by the discovery that during the night someone had painted large red crosses on both sides of the white van.

"The Road Hogs!" seethed Dennis. "It has to be them!"

"It's beautiful!" breathed Howie reverently.

"What?"

"Why didn't we think of this?" asked Sam, shaking his head. "It's so obvious."

"Now we really are the Ambulance," Sheldon confirmed.

"But guys, don't you see?" protested Dennis. "They're making fun of us!"

Sam nodded. "True. The Road Hogs are a bunch of jerks. But they did us a real favor here. It's almost a tribute."

Kevin snapped a picture of the newly decorated Ambulance.

"You may as well get used to it, Dennis," Rob sighed, running his finger across the red paint. "It's there to stay."

A tour of the Olentangy caves occupied most of the morning. Once again Kevin was not permitted to take photographs, which caused a bit of a fuss, especially when Sam tried to organize negotiations. Nick made the morning hideous with his repeated warnings that the departed Indians were displeased by the presence of tourists in the caves and there was likely a curse in effect. This scared Sheldon almost witless. Howie, having got word that there was a science museum in Columbus, paid absolutely no attention to the exhibits and devoted all his efforts to nagging. There, thought Rob, was the curse.

Dennis, of course, reserved his enthusiasm for the souvenir shop. Despite warnings of impending bankruptcy he simply could not leave without a feathered headdress, a tomahawk, a totem pole backscratcher and, on a reluctant loan from Rob, a junior folding pup-tepee. Less than a third of the way to Los Angeles, Dennis was well on his way to being broke.

In the afternoon the group voted to drive around

the city to get an overall view of the place. The tally was six to one, with one abstaining. Howie was still holding out for the science museum and Artie had no opinion, saying, "Whatever suits everybody suits me."

"Gee, the drivers around Columbus are awfully friendly," Dennis remarked as they drove into the city. "Look at how they move out of the way to let us by. Now this is courtesy."

"Not quite," said Rob drily. "I think they're pulling over because they see our red crosses."

"Excellent!" crowed Kevin. "They think we're a real ambulance!"

The boys indulged in a lively chorus of the group yell.

"Oh boy," breathed Dennis as the drivers in the road ahead glanced back, spied the van, and quickly moved over to the curb. "I hope there isn't a law against this."

"I think we're going to find out," said Rob, indicating the police car pulling alongside. The officer waved to Dennis, who waved weakly back, and then drove out in front of the white van and activated his siren. "What's he doing?" asked Dennis. "Are we under arrest?"

Through the streets of downtown Columbus raced the police cruiser, its wailing siren stopping traffic, clearing the way for the Ambulance van. Dennis and Rob looked anxiously out the front window. Rob waved frantically, trying to signal the policeman. The campers cheered enthusiastically. They followed the cruiser the wrong way down a one-way street and through a wide driveway marked by a sign which read *Columbus General Hospital.*

"Oh, no!" groaned Rob.

The policeman got out of his car and stood watching. When no white-uniformed attendants burst out of the back door carrying a stretcher, he approached the van and looked inside.

"What the—? This isn't an ambulance!"

"Oh—ha ha—of course not," said Dennis, trying to sound cheerful. "You see, we're with Juniortours and people seem to think—"

"Seems to me you've got this van painted up like an ambulance," the young officer said peevishly.

"Well, yes, we have," said Dennis, "but that's only because the name of our group is Ambulance, and you have to paint your van, and—uh—this is how we painted ours because—uh—oh, forget it."

Roll 4, exposure 31. Rob standing in line at Columbus City Hall to pay ticket.
(We were creating a public nuisance.)

While Rob and Kevin were paying the group's debt to society Dennis and the boys spray-painted white enamel over the red crosses on the Ambulance.

Sam was making a great show of not participating, as a protest against an unjust law. "Scabs!" he accused his vanmates. "We have to stand together on this thing! They have no right to make us cover up our beautiful red crosses! We've got a case here!"

"But, Sam," Dennis explained reasonably, "we have no choice. We're dealing with the police."

"We have rights," Sam insisted. "If we were

76

adults they wouldn't have made us paint out our crosses."

"Of course they would have."

"They would? Oh. Well. This isn't much, I suppose, but you have to think about where it's going to end. First they tell you how to decorate your van and the next thing you know—bang, you're a slave."

Rob didn't quote figures as he left City Hall after paying the fine, but the financial outlook for the two counselors was not rosy.

"Don't worry," smiled Dennis optimistically. "We'll do some cost-cutting in Chicago."

The power of positive parking

Bound for Interstate 65 after leaving Columbus, Dennis somehow ended up on R.R. #11 instead. The two-lane cow path wound through pleasant rural country and past prosperous farms, but clearly did not lead to Chicago. So Dennis called upon his keen native sense of direction, which led them down several dirt roads, each becoming increasingly inhospitable. The final one ended abruptly at the steep face of a gorge. This particular gorge being very beautiful, Kevin set up his tripod and began to snap nature studies while Sam, Nick, Howie and Sheldon experimented with the group yell over the echoing cliffs.

Backtracking, they asked directions of a farmer. He could not locate the highway, precisely—but wouldn't they like to see a fine field of alfalfa? Pointing out that Pete Ogrodnick had minored in agriculture at university, Sheldon accepted on behalf of the group. The field was duly admired, and the search continued. Then a thunderstorm broke, rendering the dirt roads almost impassable.

By ten o'clock at night Ambulance group, with Rob at the wheel, had reached Chicago. Dennis was buried in the enormous city map, calling out street names and directions, and the boys were all asleep.

"Late again," said Rob in disgust. "When Butcher sees our check-in time he's going to come after us with a knife. Just another little something to add to our legend."

There was a rustling in the back and Nick's head appeared between the two counselors. "It's after ten. Aren't we there yet?"

"Almost," said Rob. "Dennis got us pretty lost back there. And with that and a bit of bad luck—"

The word "luck" was out of his mouth before he realized his mistake.

"Well," said Nick immediately, "I really think you guys have been pretty careless lately, what with parking in spot 14 and all that—"

Dennis put down the map. "Look, Nick, I can see how rubbing a rabbit's foot doesn't do anybody any harm, but you can't live your whole life on superstition. I mean, it was funny the first few times, but now I think we should all forget about this 'luck' business."

Nick was silent as Rob checked into the camp and began to cruise the rows looking for a parking space. Finally, the boy could bear it no longer.

"Watch where you park."

Rob slammed on the brakes and the van jolted to

a halt. "That's it! I can't take it anymore! If you want to blame everything that's gone wrong for us on unlucky parking spaces, then let's see you do better. From now on we're going to let *you* make the luck. So sacrifice a goat, read the entrails and tell me where to park! The helm is yours!"

"Gee, that's great, Rob," said Nick, pleased.

"Hurry up!" Rob urged. "We await your decision!"

"I've got a good feeling about 35," said Nick.

"35 it is. Prepare for sunshine and roses."

* * *

The next morning when Ambulance group awoke, Rob was on top of the situation.

"All right, everybody, don't move. We've got to do this right. Nick, we're getting up. Any suggestions on how we can do it luckily?"

"Well, no, Rob, it doesn't work that way," replied Nick seriously. "There are no luck rules for something simple like getting out of bed."

"Well, I'll tell you what then. Since we're not experts we'll just follow exactly what you do. Okay, Nick. Go ahead."

There was much laughing and joking among the boys as they all tried to copy Nick's every movement in his morning routine.

Rob peppered the exercise with sarcastic refereeing. "Come on, Howie. Nick put his pants on *left* leg first." "Any special teeth we should brush first, Nick —molars, incisors?" "Is it lucky to eat corn flakes when you're parked in spot 35, Nick?" "No, no, Sheldon. Mustn't mention Pete Ogrodnick unless Nick mentions him first."

"Oh, Rob!" exclaimed Nick. "This isn't right. You're not taking it seriously. You guys can't spend the whole day doing what I do. Good luck is just taking into account certain things." From his bed-roll he produced a large, well-thumbed paperback book. "Like biorhythms. Okay, everybody, tell me your birthday and I'll check it out."

A swift examination of everyone's biorhythm chart left Nick staring at the book in amazement. "I can't believe it! Do you have any idea how good today is?"

"How good?" asked Rob skeptically.

"I've seen high ratings before, but never for eight people! I'd better chart it again. It can't be right."

He took another look at the book and then shook his head. "I wasn't wrong! We could do *anything* today! We could drive the Ambulance right up the slopes of Mount Everest!"

The group voted to go into the city instead and, as Dennis put it, "coast on the momentum of our great biorhythms." Artie was the only abstainer, saying, "I'm sure you guys will decide on something interesting."

"Come on, Artie," urged Dennis. "You're a living, breathing human being. Surely there's something you want to do. Speak up."

Artie shrugged. "Not really."

"Just in case you're getting any ideas, Artie," added Rob, "you'd better know that the very first rule of luck is that people who take off from groups with high biorhythms get run over by cement trucks."

Artie acknowledged this with a slight smile.

Dennis sidled over to Rob. "Nevin, that kid is starting to worry me," he whispered. "He's got no personality—doesn't care where we go, what we do. Let's concentrate on bringing him out today."

"*You* can worry about bringing him out," Rob whispered back, "and I'll put *my* efforts into keeping him."

Nick was still staring at his book. "I can't believe it! What incredible luck!"

* * *

The incredible luck began at a large indoor shopping complex, where Sheldon lost his balance and tumbled backwards into the decorative fountain. Nick, Sam, Howie and Kevin collapsed with laughter, and even Dennis and Rob were hard-put to hide their amusement as they fished Sheldon out of the drink.

"I guess good old Pete Ogrodnick was right when he said you were unco-ordinated!" howled Sam, and the group dissolved anew.

Dripping wet, Sheldon smiled sheepishly.

"Well, Nick," grinned Rob, "what's the story here? How can this happen with such high bio-rhythms?"

Just then the mall manager hurried up, all concern. While Dennis escorted the soggy Sheldon back to the van to change into dry clothing, the man apologized profoundly to the others. "To think that this could have happened in our mall! What you must think of us! I'm so sorry! And tourists, too!"

When Sheldon and Dennis returned, the manager took Sheldon to the barber shop to have his hair blown dry, then hustled the whole group into the photographic studio for a complimentary group portrait, frame included. He even said he'd toss in a small brass plate which was to read *Ambulance Group, 1984,* and eight wallet-size versions of the picture. Then he treated them all to chocolate milk and donuts while the photos were being developed and printed.

"What great luck!" crowed Howie as the group carried its prize back to the van. "You were right, Nick!"

Nick smiled smugly.

"He was a great photographer, too," said Kevin. "A little cranky, but with super results. I hope he didn't mind my advice."

Dennis opened the back door of the van and stowed the portrait away lovingly. "What did I tell you, guys? Amazing things happen when we pull together as a group. Right, Artie?"

"Right," said Artie blandly.

"Where to next?" asked Sam.

"Well," said Rob, "let's check with our luck consultant. Nick? Any ideas? North? South? East? West?"

"West sounds good."

"West it is," said Dennis, jumping in behind the wheel. "That'll take us right downtown. Then we can park and do the town on foot."

They drove for a while, taking in the sights and glorying in their beautiful portrait and even more beautiful luck. Suddenly Nick sat forward and cried out, "Turn right!"

"What?"

"Turn right—fast!"

"Do it!" cheered Sam, Howie, Kevin and Sheldon, who were willing to accept Nick's word for anything.

With a squeal of the tires Dennis wheeled the van around the corner into a dilapidated, rather ugly street, which stretched for about twenty yards to an abandoned furniture factory and a dead end.

"Well, this is a stroke of luck," said Rob. "We're nowhere. What was that all about?"

"I saw something run across the road ahead," Nick explained, weak with relief. "It might have been a black cat. We couldn't risk having it cross our path."

"Is that all?" snapped Dennis. "Now it's going to take me half an hour to work my way back into the traffic on the main drag."

"Why don't we eat lunch here?" said Sam. "There's a restaurant. And—hey, look!"

Just in from the corner stood Patrick's Diner. Underneath the sign was a huge banner which read:

75th Anniversary Celebration
12-1 Today Only   1909 Prices

Dennis checked his watch and smiled. "Far out! We're just in time. Good job, Nick. We're unbeatable today!"

The customers were being met at the door by Patrick himself, grandson of the original Patrick. Lunch for eight came to $2.19 with dessert, and

Ambulance group walked out of the diner stuffed to the ears and sporting buttons which read:

Patrick's Diner—Diamond Jubilee
1909-1984
Steak 23 cents

"Well, Artie, what do you think of that?" asked Dennis in delight.

"Very good," said Artie, not specifying whether he was referring to the food, the prices or the luck that had brought them there.

Deciding to leave the Ambulance where it was parked, the group embarked on a walking tour of downtown Chicago. The luck of the day seemed to be continuing, for they ran into a man from Tourism Illinois who was distributing free passes to the observation deck of the Sears Tower. The group enjoyed the view, though not as much as the ride in the high-speed elevator. Outside, a street artist decided that he simply had to draw a caricature of Artie, whose eyes intrigued him. Sam, acting as agent, refused to surrender Artie unless the rest of the group was drawn as well. A lively negotiation ensued and a deal was finally struck in which Artie would be drawn free, contingent on·the other seven being offered their pictures at half price. The group was ecstatic. The only calm member was Artie himself, who posed in complacent silence.

A while later, while touring a downtown television studio, the group was informed that there was still seating left in the studio audience for the weekly comedy show, "My Mother the Podiatrist."

Overjoyed, they settled themselves for the free entertainment.

Coming out of the show the group caught sight of an advertisement for a large amusement park just outside of town. They picked up the van and headed for the park, which, in perfect keeping with their current spell of good luck, was promoting its newest and greatest attraction, the SuperSlide, highest slide in the world. For a mere penny one could shoot the treacherous curves and thrilling hills and dips while seated on a burlap mat. The boys were delighted.

Rob was nervous. "Dennis, we can't let them go up there alone! It's a mile in the sky!"

Dennis, who was suffering from heartburn after ramming three orders of cotton candy down his throat in rapid succession, sat down heavily. "You go with them. I'll stay here with Artie—he says he'd rather sit it out too."

So Rob made endless trips up the SuperSlide's towering staircase, safeguarding the lives of his charges and shooting down the drop with them, only to have to start up again. By the time the boys had had enough, Rob had had more than enough.

As the afternoon progressed, thoughts of dinner began to develop. So the group headed back downtown to search for a restaurant worthy of this magnificent day. Rob was riding in the back of the van, leaving the navigator's seat open for Nick. The parking space that Nick selected turned out to have a broken meter, which would accept no money and which stood permanently at twenty-three minutes.

"Nice little piece of luck," said Sam smugly, coming to accept the good fortune as a matter of course.

"Okay, Nick, pick a restaurant."

Rob reached down and picked up a sheet of paper which the breeze had wafted across the street to his feet. *"Redeemable for one free regular spaghetti dinner with each one purchased. Gino's Real Italian Cuisine, 555 Market Street."* He looked at Nick suspiciously. "What are you—a witch or something?"

Gino's slogan was "the best spaghetti anywhere," and the high-flying Ambulance group was in complete agreement. They dined in economical splendor, gloating over their consistent luck. No holds were barred in praise of Nick and his biorhythms.

Leaving Gino's the group decided to stay in town for a while longer to walk off supper. They toured casually, mostly window-shopping, until the sky began to darken. When they returned to the van they found a piece of paper tucked under the windshield wiper.

"Aw, no!" moaned Dennis. "We had such a great day, and now it has to be spoiled by a parking ticket! What a drag!" Frowning in disgust, he pulled the paper from under the wiper and examined it. "Hey, wow! Get a load of this! *Congratulations! The Greater Chicago Merchants' Association is pleased to inform you that as of 8 p.m., your vehicle was parked in one of today's randomly selected Lucky Spots. To pick up your prize, come to—*I can't believe it! We've won something!"

Cheering themselves hoarse, the boys once again piled into the van and Dennis drove to the designated store.

Rob presented the ticket to the woman at the

counter, who disappeared into the back of the store for a moment and then came out carrying a small carton.

Dennis stared at the writing on the box. "A toaster?"

"Wow!" breathed Howie.

"Just what we needed!" added Kevin, capturing the magic moment on film.

Rob put his head down on the counter and laughed until tears were rolling down his cheeks.

* * *

Roll 5, exposure 31. Toaster at work.

"Come on, guys," coaxed Dennis. "No more toast. You should all be in bed."

"Just one more slice each," wheedled Howie. "It's five to twelve, and we don't want to miss one second of our day."

"I've checked around," said Sam proudly, "and we're the only group with a toaster."

"Not bad," commented Sheldon, starting on his fifth slice.

"But it's more than just a toaster," Sam continued. "Sure, it makes great toast. But more important, we won it together. It belongs to all our group. I admit I had my doubts at first, but it's starting to be pretty obvious that we're the best group on this tour."

There was general agreement.

"All right, guys," said Rob, who had not really stopped laughing since seeing the prize. "Go to sleep.

Tomorrow's another day—maybe not like this one, but we can't be greedy. We have our toaster."

When the boys were bedded down and asleep Dennis and Rob sat at the front of the van reviewing the events of their remarkable day.

"When you said we should unite this group," chuckled Rob, "I thought it couldn't be done. But if you'd told me that the whole group would rally around a toaster—"

"What a day!" breathed Dennis. "It almost makes me want to believe in this biorhythm stuff. But if the kids are happy, then I'm happy. Nevin, our troubles are over at last!"

"Big deal. You've already started making up new ones. Why did you set up a date with Kathy and Susan when you know we're running low on cash? I don't think they'll be very impressed if we take them out for a glass of water. Dennis, how could you be so stupid?"

"How could I resist? There we were—the moon, the stars and the Rhode Island Reds. They really like us, Nevin. Let the Road Hogs have Cindy and Vera. Our Reds make their Blues look like men."

"But, Dennis—"

"You'll see.

* * *

Rob came awake in the middle of the night with the strange feeling that something was amiss. He sat up in his bedroll and scanned the floor of the tent. There was one empty sleeping bag. His breath caught in his throat. Artie was gone again! But no.

Artie was there, fast asleep, his briefcase clutched to his heart. Rob saw a faint glimmer of light outside the tent and crawled out to investigate. There, sitting cross-legged on the grass, was Sheldon, examining a handful of photographs by flashlight.

"Hey, Sheldon, what are you doing up?"

The boy wore a look of deep sadness and his voice was melancholy. He pointed to the picture on top of the pile. "This is Pete and me building a snow fort a couple of winters ago. And here we are playing miniature golf in Vermont. Here's Pete with his dog, Hamlet." He sighed. "I just couldn't believe he'd go away."

"I guess you miss him a lot," said Rob sympathetically. He squinted at the pictures in the dim light. Pete Ogrodnick was just a *normal person* and, yes, even a little on the fat side. It was almost comforting.

"Here we are at an Expos game," Sheldon went on sadly. "We used to go a lot and we'd always root for the Expos. Gee, I really miss Pete."

"You know, Sheldon," said Rob, choosing his words as carefully as possible, "Pete sounds like the greatest friend a guy could ever have. But you've got to understand that friends can't always be together. You have to go on living. Didn't you have a good time today?"

Sheldon looked greatly troubled. "Today was the first day since Pete left that I hardly thought about him at all. I had so much fun. I'm really happy, but at the same time I'm really sad because Pete's gone. I think it's great that I'm a member of Ambulance group, and I like all the guys and you and Dennis, and things are going so well, what with the toaster and all that, but I feel funny that when I get home from this trip Pete won't be there."

"I think," said Rob kindly, "that Pete would be the happiest guy in the world to know that you're fitting in so well and having a good time. And when you see him again he'll be very proud of the kind of person you've become."

Sheldon turned earnest eyes to his counselor. "Really?"

"Really," said Rob, feeling for the first time the weight of his eighteen years. Here was Sheldon, the pesty kid who never shut up, turning to him in time of trouble. And he, Rob Nevin, was honestly coming up with worthwhile advice. It was astounding. With effort, he might even become as wise as—dare he say it?—Pete Ogrodnick. "And in the meantime, you shouldn't feel guilty about letting yourself go with your new friends. I mean, this tour is a really good thing. Enjoy it. Be the Ambulance. Make toast."

Sheldon brightened. "I think I understand. Yeah. Thanks, Rob."

"Any time. Now you should get some sleep."

"Okay. Would you like to look at the rest of my photos?"

"Sure," said Rob, wanting anything but. "Tomorrow, in daylight. I want to see them properly."

He sat for a few moments to allow Sheldon to get back into his bedroll and fall asleep. Well, he thought, *that* was an experience, one he never would have had painting houses in Montreal. Though, indisputably, had he taken the painting job, he wouldn't be sitting in Chicago keeping a wary eye on Artie and an even warier one on Dennis, the last of the big-time spenders.

No frills

The much-awaited date with the Rhode Island Reds was a bust. Dennis and Rob, both scrubbed, shining and drenched in after-shave, went in search of Kathy and Susan to find that the occupants of the red van were in quarantine with chicken pox. Instead of dining and dancing, Dennis and Rob were forced to be content with toast, Pete Ogrodnick and blitzkrieg nagging from Howie for a trip to the local planetarium.

Following their stay in Chicago, the Juniortours groups were all given four days of unscheduled time. It was a good thing, too, because one of Dennis's vagabond driving experiments put the Ambulance so far into the middle of nowhere that Rob had to take over the wheel. When he finally managed to locate a known highway, the group had wandered far south into the state of Missouri, just north of St. Louis. Dennis refused to pass up the opportunity to visit that fine city and rallied the support of the campers behind him.

The next few days were a blur of amusement parks, sightseeing tours and souvenir stands as the wayward Ambulance cut a joyous path across the United States several hundred miles south of their prescribed course. Had Rob not been so worried about the schedule, he would have enjoyed himself more. The group was on a roll, and spirits were high. Even Artie had been a model of behavior lately. It was starting to look as if Dennis was right and Artie had settled down. He'd even bought himself a little souvenir, a ninety-five-cent pamphlet entitled *Dairy Farming in Nebraska*—a peculiar choice for a memento, but then Artie wasn't your average kid.

Still, one could never be too careful. "It's not that I don't have faith in you, Artie," Rob commented somewhere between St. Louis and Kansas City, "but just in case you have any plans for some disappearances in the next little while, I'd like to point out that we will be in Ogallala, Nebraska. Do you know what's in Ogallala, Nebraska, Artie?"

Artie looked politely interested.

"Nothing!" exclaimed Rob, smiling broadly. "Nil, naught, zero, zilch, the empty set. Not a sausage. There is absolutely no reason for you to disappear, because no matter where you go, you're still in the same place. Nowhere. Not only that, but we're going to be staying way out of the town, such as it is."

"It should be a nice change," said Artie blandly.

The day the group was due to check in at Ogallala the van's radiator boiled over, knocking Dennis's tight timetable right into left field. He bounced back, though, with five hundred uninterrupted miles of frantic driving through blistering heat to arrive at the trailer park a full eight minutes before deadline.

* * *

"Hello, everybody, and welcome to beautiful Lake McConaughy." Charlie Butcher smiled benignly down on the entire Juniortours assembly. Taking a deep breath, he began his yearly spiel. "This is our big event, the old Double-J Juniortours Jamboree. You've all been touring around pretty much on your own, but here's where we all come together—the ones who started out in New York, Los Angeles, Houston, Miami—and you Canadian guys. The next few days we're going to be having sports and games and good old healthy competition. There'll be fishing, boating and water-skiing. There'll be marshmallow roasts and sing-songs. We're all going to be one big happy family!"

"Do you think we look like we've got six kids?" Rob whispered to Dennis as Butcher raved on. Artie had disappeared without a trace an hour after breakfast.

* * *

"Let me get this straight, kid," said the farmer, looking across his kitchen table at the young boy in the tuxedo. "You want to *rent* six of my cows?"

"For three days," Artie confirmed. "Naturally, they'll be stabled with you at night. I'll need them from about six to ten in the morning and six to ten in the evening."

One of the farmer's daughters, a girl of eighteen,

brought them each a tall glass of apple cider. "Daddy, are you all right?" she asked her father, who was looking quite pale.

He nodded absently. "What are you going to do with six cows?"

"Milk them," said Artie. "And if you don't mind I'd prefer six high-yield, docile cows."

The farmer looked Artie straight in the eye. "Each of my cows gives about two gallons of milk twice a day. Six cows gives you twenty-four gallons. What are you going to do with twenty-four gallons of milk? Take a bath?"

Artie smiled. "You just leave that to me, sir. Here's my offer. You give me six good unmilked cows at the times I need them for the next three days, and I'll pay you five hundred dollars, cash."

The farmer's eyes bulged. "Where's a little shaver like you going to get five hundred dollars?"

"In advance," Artie added, making an elaborate show of pulling the key from his pouch and opening his briefcase. He counted out five crisp hundred-dollar bills.

The farmer shook his head. "Listen, kid. I'm not an idiot. The only way you can make back five hundred dollars on my cows is to sell them. And then where would I be?"

"You'll have to trust me," said Artie. "I won't do anything dishonest."

"How about I send my daughter along to make sure you don't do anything wrong or mistreat my cattle?"

"Certainly," Artie agreed readily.

"I'm interested to see how you're going to make

any money out of this," said the farmer. "All right, kid. It's a deal." He shook his head, muttering, "I can't believe it!"

* * *

When Artie returned to the group just before supper he found Rob smug rather than angry.

"Back so soon? I guess you found out that there isn't very much going on around here."

Artie smiled. "I guess not."

Rob laughed. "This is one time that, if I asked you what you'd been doing and you said 'nothing,' I'd believe it. Didn't I tell you about Ogallala? I'm not going to ask you where you were because I know you won't tell me. But you'd better believe that if you try to take off one more time you'll be bound and gagged and thrown under the van until we leave. Is that clear?"

Artie nodded mildly.

That evening the entire Juniortours group held a mammoth bonfire and marshmallow roast on the beach of Lake McConaughy. Butcher was host, moving from party to party, radiating good will and bluff charm. It was an act, of course, since Butcher loathed the great outdoors. He didn't even eat marshmallows, having been told by his doctor years ago that he had a choice of giving up either sweets or beer.

The party ran long into the night. At twelve o'clock the campers all went to their tents, but some of the counselors, Dennis and Rob included, stayed out on the beach.

In the Ambulance tent, the group was getting ready for bed.

"Would anyone be interested in a little business proposition?"

The boys lapsed into a shocked silence. *Artie Geller was speaking to them!* This was the first time on the entire trip that Artie had actually initiated a conversation.

Sam was the first to recover. "A business proposition?"

"Yes," said Artie. "It's a little idea I've been toying with, and I'm going to need some help. You'll be paid, of course."

The agent in Sam was aroused. "How much?"

"Fifty dollars each."

The boys were impressed.

"But, Artie," said Sheldon, "where are you going to get that kind of money? Dennis and Rob have been paying for you the whole trip. They say you spent all your money in New York."

"Let me worry about that," said Artie with a smile of quiet confidence.

"Gee," said Howie, "I've never been in business before. What kind of business is it?"

Artie leaned closer and dropped his voice. "Agricultural."

There was another shocked silence, so Artie specified: "We're in cows."

* * *

At four o'clock in the morning the six members of Ambulance group slipped out of camp, leaving their counselors fast asleep. Overawed, they followed the tuxedo-clad Artie to a remote section of the park where a row of six abandoned outdoor changing booths, sadly in need of paint, still stood. These had been in use when the waters of Lake McConaughy were higher, for then they had stood only fifty feet from the beach. But the lake had receded considerably since then, and the booths were now out of the way and forgotten.

Sam hefted the van's tool box and distributed screwdrivers all around, and the boys set to work removing the wooden doors.

From the inside pocket of his jacket Artie produced a sheet of paper and handed it to Nick. "These are the painting instructions," he said. "You can use the cans of spray paint I've brought along—the ones we got in New York when we painted the name on the van. Make sure you do all the signs exactly the way I've got the wording here."

"You know," said Sam, "if we do the signs ourselves they aren't going to look very good."

"What we're working on is a no-frills business," Artie explained. "Fancy signs would be frills. Now, don't talk to anybody if you're approached. I'll be gone for a while to get our cattle."

Howie's eyes grew wide like saucers. "You're bringing cows *here?*"

"Well, of course," Artie replied. "This is a no-frills milk store, and milk that's already out of the cow is a frill. Our customers are going to do it themselves."

*   *   *

Angie, the farmer's daughter who had served the

apple cider the previous day, and her seventeen-year-old sister, Linda, were waiting for Artie with six Jersey cows.

"See, Linda? I told you. A little guy in a tuxedo." She turned to Artie. "My dad says we both have to go with you to watch out for the cows."

"That's fine," said Artie. He motioned back towards the trailer park. "Shall we go?"

The three walked along, driving the cows ahead of them. Artie, reticent as always, said nothing. The girls were chatty.

"Okay," said Angie, "the deal's made, so you can tell us now. How are you going to make money from these cows?"

"I'm going to sell the milk," Artie explained.

"But you won't have five-hundred dollars' worth," put in Linda.

"Yes I will. It's a simple matter of reduced quantities and increased prices."

Both girls stared at him. "And you expect to have customers?"

Artie just smiled.

When they arrived at the campsite everything was ready. Sam, Nick, Howie, Kevin and Sheldon were sitting in front of the change booths under an enormous sign which read in crude letters:

NO-FRILLS MILK STORE
TIME-SHARING PROGRAM: $1. per
COW MINUTE (NO COINS, PLEASE)
B.Y.O.B. (BRING YOUR OWN BUCKET)
HOURS: 7-9:30 a.m and 7-9:30 p.m. daily

All around the trailer camp—except for the Juniortours section—were smaller signs saying *No-
Frills Milk Store* with arrows pointing towards the
makeshift stalls. Artie glanced at his five helpers
with approval. As per instructions, each one now
sported a white T-shirt with the inscription *Cow
Expert* written in black magic marker across the
front.

"Okay," said Artie. "I need one cow per stall,
facing the rear."

The two girls stared. Above each stall was a
name. The cows were now Georgette, Babette, Colette, Suzette, Mariette and Annette.

"That was my idea," said Nick proudly. "It's bad
luck to have a cow without a name." He added
nervously, "It's all right, isn't it, Artie?"

Artie nodded. "Okay, man your stations. I think
we've got customers coming."

"You mean," said Linda incredulously, "that you
expect people to pay you a buck to milk a cow for
one lousy minute? Why, an inexperienced milker
won't get more than a couple of ounces!"

Artie nodded. "I costed it at three."

The Juniortours people accounted for less than a
quarter of the population of the huge state park, so
many of the early risers were camping families with
younger children. True to Artie's plan, the first customers came at precisely seven o'clock. It was a
family consisting of a mother, father and three children, one a baby.

"Hey, now, what's all this about?" the man asked
Artie.

"It's a no-frills milk store," Artie explained.

"Need any milk?"

"Okay," said the man. "How much for a quart?"

"It varies," Artie replied. "How good a milker are you?"

"What?"

"Well, if we sold the milk already out of the cow, that would be a frill. In our no-frills time-sharing program, you rent time on one of our quality, Grade A, government-inspected milk cows, and do the milking yourself."

The man looked up and read the sign. "A dollar a minute, huh? That's a pretty good idea. Okay, you're on." He held out a dollar.

"Do you have a bucket?" Artie inquired.

"You mean you don't supply buckets?"

"Oh no, sir. That would be a frill."

"I'll go bring a pot, Daddy!" said the man's little girl excitedly.

"Good idea," said her father. "Make sure you get a big one."

The girl ran off. By now a good number of people were circulating about the compound, and a crowd of the curious was gathering around the No-Frills Milk Store. The little girl quickly returned, struggling under the weight of an enormous stewpot.

"Here, Daddy."

"Okay, kid, here goes." The man entered the stall, placing the pot under Annette and sitting down on the small built-in bench.

Artie regarded his watch. "Okay—go!"

The man began milking furiously, egged on by the cheers of his children and the other spectators. His expression was intense, his hands worked like pistons, and sweat soon covered his body.

Artie called "Time!" and the man leaned back, exhausted, amid great applause from the ever-increasing crowd. He looked down into the pot. A thin film of white milk partially covered the large bottom.

"Hey, wait a minute!" he bawled. "Where's all the milk?"

The crowd broke into laughter and six eager people came forward to Artie with money and buckets, anxious to try their hands. Artie gently coaxed the bewildered man out of the stall, and the five cow experts set up the six new milkers, one per cow. A line-up began to form.

"But I didn't even get a thimble-ful!" complained the first man, still staring with disbelief into his stewpot.

"You're welcome to rent some more time, sir. Just step to the end of the line, please. We're very busy here." Artie turned back to the stalls. "Okay—go!"

Now the cheering was tumultuous as the six milkers raced furiously against time for their dollar's worth. The noise of the crowd attracted so many more people that there was a long line-up and an enormous crowd when Artie finally called, "Time!"

In Suzette's booth a woman screamed. "I didn't get any!" she wailed to Sam as he escorted her out to make room for a young boy who was eager to try it next.

"Never mind, lady," soothed Sam. "Uh—I didn't do very well my first time either. And look at me now." He thrust his chest out proudly. "I'm a cow expert."

"Okay," called Artie. "Go!"

As the cheering began again and the six milkers

threw themselves into their work Angie and Linda approached Artie. "I don't get it!" Angie exclaimed. "Why would all these people be so willing to pay a dollar for one minute on a cow? They know they're not getting any milk."

Artie shrugged. "Country people wouldn't pay it," he said, his eyes never leaving his watch, "but these are all city people. City people are the ones who go camping. Country people go to the city for vacations."

"Well, our father is going to have a fit when we tell him about this!" Linda predicted. "He might not even believe us! You're going to be rich!"

Artie smiled. "Time!" he called.

"I got more than you!" one boy shouted at his sister.

"No, I got more!"

Sheldon interjected diplomatically, "I think you both got exactly the same amount."

"How would you know?"

Sheldon pointed to his shirt. "We cow experts can always tell."

"Move it along, please," Artie urged. "Okay, next group. Is everybody ready? Go!"

* * *

So it was that at a quarter after eight that morning Dennis and Rob woke up to an empty tent.

"Oh, no!" moaned Rob. "The kids are gone!"

Dennis was calm. "Take it easy. There's no place for them to go. You said so yourself."

Suddenly the sound of faraway cheering reached

Rob's ears. He and Dennis dressed madly and ran across the park in the direction of the commotion. An extraordinary sight met their eyes. At the site of the old wooden change rooms was a sea of people, hundreds of them, milling around, craning their necks, flailing their arms and shouting. Great waves of laughter mingled with the cheers. Jutting out from the mob was a long line of people stretching across the compound, all the way to the rows of parked vehicles. Those in the line all seemed to be carrying pots, pans and pails, and new people were constantly arriving.

Dennis stared. "What is it?"

"I don't know," said Rob grimly, "but I've got a *really* bad feeling about it, whatever it is. Come on."

The two counselors scrambled over to the crowd. Rob elbowed his way to the front. He spied his tuxedo-clad charge and his jaw dropped. He closed his eyes and opened them again. Yes, Artie was still there at the centre of whatever it was, dressed like a head waiter and obviously in charge. Unable to think of anything to say, Rob concentrated on volume rather than meaning.

"Artie!"

"I'll handle this," said Sam to Artie. "Cow expert, sir. What seems to be the—oh, hi, Rob."

Artie called "Time" and the cow experts cleared the booths and rushed in the next six milkers.

Rob stalked over to Artie. "Artie Geller, what *is* this?"

"Pardon me, Rob? Oh, *this*. This is a no-frills milk store."

"Yes, I know! I can read! But where do you fit in? Whose store is it?"

Artie shrugged. "Nobody's."

"Don't give me that! Come away from here this minute! When we get back to the van you can take off that ridiculous suit!"

"Okay—go!" called Artie. To Rob he added, "I can't leave."

"You can if I pick you up and haul you away! Now move!"

"Hey, bud," came a gruff voice from the line, "get out of here! Can't you see the kid's busy?"

Rob had a brief, giddy vision of Artie's pamphlet, *Dairy Farming in Nebraska,* and a horrible thought began to ease its way into his mind. His voice became less authoritative and more edgy. "This is all a joke, right, Artie? I mean, you and the other kids got together and are doing this for some farmer who's letting you hang around, right? Right?"

"If you say so, Rob. Oh, excuse me. *Time!*"

Just then Dennis arrived on the scene. "Well, Rob, what do you think of Artie's no-frills milk store? I think it's all pretty slick," he said proudly.

Rob didn't answer. With a sinking heart he looked at the large box of incoming cash sitting on the ground in front of Artie. "So, you—*own* all this?" he asked faintly.

"Oh, no," said Artie. "The cows are rented. Next group—go!"

The cheering of the crowd around him was making Rob dizzy. "But Artie!" he blustered. "You only had fifteen cents!"

From the line two girls, both Juniortours counselors, approached Artie.

"Excuse me—we saw a kid in New York wearing a

tuxedo just like yours, selling attack jelly on the boardwalk at Coney Island. He was about your size too."

Rob stifled a cry of shock. Dennis goggled.

"Really?" said Artie politely.

"Yeah. He was making a fortune, just like you're doing here. Do you two know each other or something?"

"I work alone," said Artie.

"Beatrice said she saw another one in Washington," said the second girl. "A kid in a tuxedo just like this one. He was making a killing with a racing casino on Capitol Hill. I wonder what the connection is. There must be one."

"It's—it's a national network!" Rob blurted suddenly. If these girls connected Artie with Juniortours, he thought desperately, the no-frills milk would really hit the fan. "Yeah! Lots of little kids in tuxedos doing things like this all over the country! Didn't you read the article in—uh—*Business Week?*"

The girls were wide-eyed. "Really? Wow. Somebody must be making a lot of money from this. Attack jelly was just brilliant."

"Brilliant!" agreed Rob. "Why, we saw one in Pittsburgh too, didn't we, Dennis?"

Pop-eyed, Dennis nodded wordlessly.

"What was that one selling?" asked the first girl.

"Selling?" echoed Rob. "Oh yeah—selling. He was selling—volcano insurance. Isn't that right, Dennis?"

Dennis said nothing.

"Well, it's certainly very impressive," both girls agreed, and returned to their place in line.

Rob's face radiated absolute rage. All this time he had been yearning to know what Artie was doing during his disappearances. He had been fatherly, honestly concerned about the boy's welfare. And little Artie had been going into business—big business. Little Artie was rich. And now little Artie was going to *die!*

Dennis intercepted Rob's lunge. "Nevin, are you crazy?" he whispered hoarsely. "Control yourself! Now, Artie, you know we're very proud of you for all this great stuff you've been doing, but you have to understand why Rob is a little upset."

"A little *upset?*" The words came out strangled as Rob attempted to shout and whisper at the same time. "Dennis, we've got the goods on him! He's been identified selling attack jelly!" He turned his eyes heavenward and threw up his arms. "What the blazes is attack jelly?"

"Oh, nothing," said Artie. "Time!"

He looked at his counselors, one anxious, the other seething with rage. "Rob, Dennis, there's some people I want you to meet. Just let me get this next group started. Ready?" he called to his cow experts. "Okay, go!" He led Rob and Dennis over to the farmer's two daughters. "Angie, Linda, I'd like you to meet Dennis and Rob, my counselors."

Rob's look of severity began to soften. He glanced at Dennis, whose eyes were glazing over, and searched his mind for an intelligent, urbane remark. It was "Hi."

Both girls smiled warmly. Artie, his attack jelly, his casino, his milk store and his money began to fade away from the minds of the two counselors.

Artie, having set the wheels in motion, returned to business.

"So," said Dennis, grinning foolishly, "uh—how did you get to meet our Artie?"

"We live on a farm near here," said Angie. "He rented the cows from our father."

"He's an amazing little kid," said Linda.

Rob swallowed a sarcastic retort and choked out, "Oh, yes, we're very proud of him." He waited for lightning to strike him down.

"Well, we're going to be hanging around Lake Mc—" Dennis's tongue twisted. "Uh—hanging around here for the next three days, and with our kids in business, you know, it leaves us kind of at loose ends."

"Well, we'd be happy to show you around the area," Linda offered.

"Sure!" agreed Rob. He caught a sideways look from Dennis which seemed to say he had agreed much too enthusiastically for the suave, devil-may-care image Dennis would have liked to project. Well, Dennis wasn't exactly playing hard to get either!

"Why don't you stay here for lunch?" Dennis suggested. "I'm sure Juniortours can spare a few extra hot dogs, and afterwards maybe we can go to the beach and—"

"Well," said Angie, "we're supposed to stay with the cows. They have to be back home by ten."

"We'll go with you," Rob decided. "That is, we'll help you get the cows home. Okay?" he added hopefully.

Both girls laughed. "Okay."

They kept talking as Artie and his five cow experts processed hundreds of eager milkers just a short distance away. At quarter past nine Mariette began to run dry, and at twenty past, Artie closed for the morning.

"Don't worry, people," he announced to the disappointed customers who had not made it to the front of the line. "We open again at seven tonight. Thank you for your patronage."

* * *

The next morning Dennis and Rob were up before the crack of dawn to fetch the cows—and also Angie and Linda. This allowed Artie and the other campers to catch a little extra sleep and enjoy a leisurely breakfast of toast before the opening of the milk store.

At seven they launched into the new day's business with the usual vigor and enthusiasm. Interest in the milk store had not waned. Repeat customers now had their own favorite cows and were eagerly greeted by Artie and the cow experts. Little milking rivalries began to spring up, leading to contests and, ultimately, side bets. Artie did nothing to discourage this—it was good for business. And his cow experts were always there to provide service for the eager customers.

"I didn't get any milk!"

"If at first you don't succeed, try, try again. That's cow expert talk."

"Look at how little I got!"

"You did quite well, ma'am. Take it from me. I'm a cow expert."

110

"This cow is *defective!*"

"Certainly not, sir. Annette is one of the best."

"Well, you should know. You're the cow expert."

"Time!"

By now Dennis and Rob were spending much of their free time with Angie and Linda. Rob felt an occasional twinge when he thought about Artie. After all, he knew he'd have to confront him sometime. After much confused soul-searching he decided to wait until the group left Ogallala—then he'd really let Artie have it. In the meantime at least he knew where Artie was, and the other campers seemed to love being cow experts. And of course, he said to himself, one shouldn't over-supervise eleven-year-olds. Eleven-year-olds were men.

Rob's central worry remained the chance that Butcher would get close enough to the milk store to connect it with Ambulance group. In fact, he needn't have worried, since it would never have occurred to Butcher to examine the milk store from close up. To his way of thinking, milk came from sterilized glass bottles which appeared every other morning by the door of one's high-rise apartment. Butcher never bothered with anything that was obviously none of his concern.

* * *

Roll 9, exposure 23. Suzette, the most beautiful cow in the world.

Roll 9, exposure 24. Annette, almost as good as Suzette.

In between milkings the group participated under

the proud Ambulance name in the Jamboree's soccer tournament, but were knocked out in the first round by the Road Hogs. Then they tried their hand at horseshoe-pitching but were disqualified when Nick attempted to steal one of the horseshoes to hang over his bed at home. They fared no better at shuffleboard because Sam, who had a heavy hand, kept heaving the discs clear onto the other courts, creating chaos, confusion and sore ankles.

By the final day at Lake McConaughy the group was perfectly attuned to its milk store schedule. Attendance was record-breaking. The words *Last Day* had been added to the sign, and customers flocked to get their final shot at Georgette, Babette, Colette, Suzette, Mariette and Annette. Artie and his cow experts were now truly proficient at processing milkers, and functioned like a well-oiled machine.

"I can't believe it," Sam was saying mournfully as the boys ate their toast. "Only one more milking to go."

Sheldon shook his head. "Being a cow expert is without a doubt the most wonderful experience of my life. If only Pete could see me now."

"There's something special about it, all right," said Howie.

"It's a position of respect," agreed Sam. "Cow experts are somebodies. You spend your whole life being told, 'Do this,' 'Don't do that,' 'Go to bed,' 'Get up,' 'Do your homework,' and suddenly you're right up there with the big shots."

"Well," said Artie, "I think now is a good time to pay your salaries."

"It's almost hard to believe that we get paid for this," said Howie. "Being a cow expert is a privilege."

"You've earned it," Artie said approvingly.

"I've got to get a shot of this!" exclaimed Kevin, rubbing his hands together with glee. "Hold it. Stay exactly where you are. I've just got to check my light meter."

"You know, Artie," said Sam as they posed, "I feel kind of guilty about it now, but I've got to admit that at first I thought you were a bit of a creep—no offense. But now that it's obvious what a cool guy you are—I mean, this group has no flaws. I knew we were good, but now I know we're great!"

* * *

The final engagement of the no-frills milk store was a memorable occasion. The arrival of the cows was greeted with cheers and applause, and the crowd of avid fanatics chanted the animals' names as they were led into their stalls. The farmer himself had come to witness this final milking. His daughters had told him in great detail what was going on, and yet he stood in mute shock watching hundreds of people stand in line for the privilege of paying a dollar to milk, incompetently and awkwardly, one of his cows—for sixty seconds! Each milker was cheered on by the rooting of the crowd, and after finishing was met by handshakes, kisses and pats on the back. The whole thing was pure chaos, and yet hundreds of customers managed to get processed quickly and efficiently.

There was genuine sadness when the cows began to run dry and Artie declared the milk store officially closed. Strangely, no one left. The entire crowd stayed and watched as the cows were led out of their stalls.

The farmer approached Artie and man and boy shook hands. "Kid," began the farmer, wracking his brain for the right words, "you're—" He looked at Artie for a long time, then shook his head and walked away.

There was a round of sincere applause as Sam and Nick took down the big sign.

* * *

At two o'clock in the morning Dennis and Rob were still awake, sitting on the grass in front of their van and talking.

"This has been a great three days," Dennis decided. "Angie and Linda are just fantastic."

"Mmmm," said Rob.

"In fact, I don't know if I've ever met two people who have more going for them. They're smart, they're nice, they're friendly—not to mention great looking. I bet they're better looking than anyone on this tour."

"The Rhode Island Reds are pretty nice," said Rob reflectively.

Dennis made a face. "The Rhode Island Reds are men! Angie and Linda blow them right off the map."

"Mmmm."

"What's with you, Nevin? We both just had the

114

greatest three days of the whole summer and you look like somebody's died."

"I'm just thinking, that's all," said Rob.

"About what?"

"Artie."

"What about him?"

"What about him? How can you say 'What about him?' Dennis, don't you realize that in New York and Washington, while we ran around looking for him, Artie was off making thousands of dollars just like he did here? You know, as soon as we said goodbye to Angie and Linda tonight I started feeling really strange about this whole thing, and I did a bit of asking around. What he did in New York and Washington is not to be believed! I've *seen* attack jelly, and let me tell you, Dennis, if you saw it you'd die! The guys I talked to paid ten dollars for theirs and thought they were getting a great deal. And the people who were at his casino on Capitol Hill say they've never seen anything like it. Dennis, they felt privileged to lose money to that kid!"

Dennis shook his head in admiration. "He's amazing!"

"I've got a better word for him—*rich!* We were so thrilled with Angie and Linda that we didn't think about how much money this kid must have! Now we know why he eats and sleeps with his briefcase—it's crammed full of money—money and a tuxedo! The only difference between Jesse James and Artie is that Jesse James had a horse. Dennis, do you realize what kind of a *mind* he must have to think up all these scams? How can we deal with a mind like that? We're just normal guys!"

"Nevin, calm down. You're getting all upset."

"Of course I'm upset! Think about what would happen if Butcher found out about even one-tenth of all this! Aside from being irrational and immoral it's probably also illegal! Dennis, one of our kids is a big-time crook and we didn't even know about it until *Nebraska!*"

"Shhh, Rob, you're shouting."

"I've got something to shout about! What are we going to do with him? He's not just taking a piece of America home with him—if we don't stop him he's going to get it all!"

One of the Road Hogs poked his head out of his tent. "Hey, you! Shut up! You're supposed to be an ambulance, not a foghorn!"

"Sorry," mumbled Dennis. "Nevin, are you all right?"

"Yeah," Rob muttered, shaking his head. "I still can't believe charging a dollar for a dribble of milk."

"Hey, don't worry about it," said Dennis. "In the morning everything'll look brighter. We'll talk about it then."

As always Dennis slept the sleep of the untroubled. Rob tossed and turned, unable to get comfortable. Finally he drifted into an uneasy slumber and uneasy dreams.

The world was experiencing a great economic crisis. No one had any more money—Artie had it all. The papers put the blame squarely on Artie's counselors. Rob peeked out his window to look down on angry demonstrators screaming for the blood of himself and Dennis, and a few were stirring an

116

enormous vat of boiling tar beside a large pile of feathers.

"Artie, do you have everybody's money?"

A shrug.

"Where did you get it all?"

"Nowhere."

"You two Canadian Ambulance guys have really done it this time!" thundered Butcher's voice.

"Better call an ambulance!" jeered the Road Hogs.

The demonstrators began to rush the door. Only one man could save the day.

"Look—up in the sky! It's a bird! It's a plane! No, it's Pete Ogrodnick!"

"The world needs its money back!" thundered Pete in a booming voice. Taking three powerful strides forward he grasped Artie's bulging attaché case and opened it to the wind. There was a clap of thunder and a flash of lightning, and the green of money filled the air. The demonstrators broke into applause and the band played "Happy Days are Here Again." Rob cheered himself hoarse.

"Geez, Rob, quiet down!" said Dennis, shaking his partner. "You'll wake up the kids!"

The Denver Twist

With Rob at the wheel the group headed off for their next stop, Denver. As he drove his anger swelled and he was unable to contain himself any longer.

"All right, Geller, this is it! You're rich, aren't you? Admit it! You're rich!"

"Of course not," said Artie.

"Well, then, how much money do you have?"

"Who can tell?"

"It must be a fortune!"

"What's money these days?"

"Look," said Rob, "I'm not an idiot. You were charging people a dollar a crack to milk those cows, and you processed thousands of customers."

Artie looked blank. "Who's counting?"

"Well, how much money did you make?" Rob persisted.

"Not much."

"Thousands of people at a buck a shot? How can it be 'not much'?"

"Overhead."

Rob slumped back in his seat. "You've got more than ten thousand dollars, haven't you, Artie?"

Artie looked vague. In fact, he knew himself to be well over the sixteen thousand dollar mark.

* * *

They made Denver a little after noon on Tuesday, checked in at the trailer camp just outside town and began their stay, as had become their custom, with a walking tour of the downtown area. There was some brief excitement when Artie disappeared, but Rob caught up with him a few minutes later in a nearby bank, converting the spoils of the no-frills milk store into larger, more portable bills.

Then the tour continued and everyone relaxed. That was a mistake because fifteen minutes later Artie was gone for real.

"How could he have gone?" Rob protested. "We were all together!"

"I don't know," shrugged Dennis. "He was just walking with us, reading through his newspaper, and suddenly he wasn't there anymore."

"He must have something to do," decided Nick. "He's a pretty important guy, you know."

Rob groaned. "What are we going to do now?" he asked.

* * *

The Twister Pretzel Factory, located in the Denver suburb of Glendale, was a large gray brick building that looked all but deserted. The decision to close up the Denver plant had come from head office in New York on Friday, and as Tuesday wound down towards that final five o'clock the disheartened workers coming off the last shift were mostly idle, watching the clock.

Catherine Finch, secretary to the Denver general manager, was the last employee left in the office area of the factory. She was sitting at a desk in the secretarial pool, sniffling a little into a handkerchief, when what seemed to her to be the company's last visitor—a young boy in a tuxedo—came in through the glass doors.

"Excuse me," said Artie politely. "I'd like to see whoever's in charge here."

Miss Finch shook her head sadly. "No one's in charge," she said, indicating the vacant office suites with a flutter of her handkerchief. "They've all gone. There's just me, and maybe ten or eleven men in the plant." She looked at the clock. "And in five minutes we'll be gone too."

"Well, in that case," said Artie, "you're in charge. Would you ask the men to come up here for a moment, please? I have a business proposition."

She stared. "You? I mean—uh—" She hit an intercom button. "Joe, could you please bring everyone up here?"

"What for?" came a voice.

She looked at Artie. "Uh—you'll have to see for yourself."

A few moments later the foreman, followed by ten plant workers, entered the office and stared at Artie.

"Hello, gentlemen," he said. "I'll get right to the

point. Do any of you have immediate plans for the future?"

There was an uncomfortable silence.

"Fine," said Artie. "Management has no further use for this building and they've left it for you to close up, I understand. I would like to delay that closing until Saturday and keep all of you on until that time."

There was a chorus of voices. "*You?*"

Joe the foreman spoke up. "Kid, I'm sure you can understand that we've got no sense of humor today. So you'd better not be joking. What exactly is there for us in this plan of yours?"

"In exchange for your services today, tomorrow, Thursday and all day and all night Friday, I'm prepared to pay each of you one-and-a-half times your normal week's pay."

There was an interested murmur among the employees.

Joe spoke again. "Forgive me for being skeptical, kid, but why should we believe you can pay us?"

"Sorry," said Artie. "I forgot to mention the terms of payment—half in cash right now on your signature saying you'll work for me, and the other half, also in cash, on Friday night. Oh, and one more thing. Your jobs will extend from running the factory to helping with incoming material to painting and even dusting and sweeping up. We're a small operation, so you'll have to do whatever needs to be done. You're all-purpose workers. Now, are you with me?"

There was a strained silence.

"Well," Artie went on, "I have the contracts and

the money in my attaché case. I await your decision." He walked into a plush private office and sat down at the desk.

The group murmured together for a while and then Joe led the procession into the office. "Okay, I've talked it over with Miss Finch and the men, and we're just crazy enough to go along with you. Uh—what do we call you? I mean, you're our boss and all that . . . "

Artie shrugged. "It doesn't matter. Call me Artie. That'll do. But don't give that name to anyone. We're *A*, that's all, just the letter *A*, and what we're doing here is top secret. That's another part of the deal."

"Okay," said Miss Finch, "but before we sign, I think I speak for everyone here when I ask just what all this is for."

Artie smiled. "You are now employees of The Pretzel, the most chic discotheque in the world."

* * *

"Something's happened to him!" moaned Rob as the group sat in the trailer park watching the sun set over the Rocky Mountains. "He always comes back! Why didn't he come back this time? Where can he be?"

"Take it easy, Nevin. He'll be back."

But Rob could see that Dennis too was feeling the strain. His partner was glancing at the time constantly and looking towards the entrance gate of the park. Only the campers were unperturbed. They were arm-wrestling and finding, with some shock, that Sheldon was the strongest among them.

"The poor kid," Rob continued anxiously. "It's all my fault. I should have watched him more closely. I should have paid more attention, and now—"

A nearby pay phone rang sharply.

"I'll get it," called Howie, running to answer it.

"Hey, wait a minute," said Rob. "That's not our call. Howie, no!"

"Hello?" said Howie. "Oh, sure. Just a minute." He held out the receiver. "Dennis, it's for you."

"For me?" asked Dennis in perplexity. "Who knows me in Denver?" He walked over and took the receiver from Howie. "Hello? . . . Yes . . . *A*? Who's *A*? Oh, you mean Artie? Sure, put him on."

By this time Rob was beside him, wringing his hands in agony. "What's going on?"

Dennis shrugged. "Some lady says she's going to connect me to Artie. Oh, hi, Artie. Where are you? . . . Uh huh—"

"Where is he?" cried Rob.

"No place," Dennis reported. "Listen, Artie, when are you coming back?" He turned to Rob. "He says he'll be gone a couple more days."

"*What?* Give me that phone! Artie, what the blazes is going on?"

"Hi, Rob," came Artie's voice.

"Have you gone insane? Tell us where you are and we'll pick you up right away!"

"I can't do that, Rob."

"*What?* Why not?"

"I can't spare the time. But don't worry. You go on with your tour of Denver and I'll meet up with you later."

"Artie, this is crazy! Where will you sleep?"

"I've made arrangements. Say hello to the other guys. 'Bye."

"Now, wait just one minute! Artie! Artie?" He turned a white face to Dennis and the rest. "He hung up!"

"Boy," said Howie, "he must be doing something really important if he can't come back to the Ambulance to sleep. Maybe even more important than cows."

Rob held his head. "What did I do to deserve this?"

"Maybe you walked under a ladder," suggested Nick.

"We'll keep a stiff upper lip and carry on," decided Dennis. "That's all we *can* do."

"We've got to find him," Rob moaned. "Can you imagine what Butcher will do to us if we show up in Albequerque without Artie?"

* * *

Artie glanced with a critical eye around the pretzel plant. "Now this," he said to his crew, "is perfect. Good size for a disco, nice high ceiling—the acoustics could be better, but we can compensate with the sound system. Naturally we'll have to lose some of those machines in the middle there."

"Lose them?" cried Joe in alarm. "Those are eight-ton pieces of equipment! They don't lose easily!"

"They'll have to be moved to the side," Artie continued. "They're right in the middle of the dance floor."

"How are we going to do that?"

Artie looked at him. "You're the foreman. I'm sure you'll work it out. Now, I like the general look of this place." He began to walk through the building, his crew of eleven following him. "You know, the concrete walls, the pipes—that sort of thing. But it's too dirty and dusty. I want you men to hose down the whole room and repaint the place a glossy black. Got it?"

"Yeah," mumbled Joe.

Artie moved over to a section of the factory where a wide conveyor belt cut the corner of the room. "Now, this part," he said, "I like. When we're in business, I want our patrons to be able to come over to this belt and help themselves to a hot pretzel fresh out of the oven. By the way, where is the oven?"

"In the next room," said a small man who had been the chief baker.

"Yes, well, I think we should move it out here so our guests can see the whole pretzel-making process."

Joe sighed. "You're the boss, Artie."

"All this has to be done right away, of course," Artie added, "so the paint will be dry when we start the decorating. Oh, and one more thing." He started to move briskly towards the office. "When our publicity starts to circulate we can expect people nosing around. Make sure no one who doesn't have business here gets in." He marched off through the door into the office, then turned and said, "The paint should be here already," and disappeared into the office, calling, "Miss Finch."

She looked up from her desk. "Yes, Artie?"

"I'd like you to go to the telegraph office for me,

please." From his pocket he produced a long list of names and addresses. "Send the following telegram to this list of people. *You are invited to The Pretzel, Friday, July 27th, 10:30 p.m. Dress optional. 5000 Gregor Avenue, Glendale, (303) 639-5000.* Sign it, *A., Denver.*"

"Will do," said Miss Finch. She stared at the list. "But Artie, these are all famous movie stars!"

"Oh, no," said Artie. "There are also a few astronauts, sports figures, film directors, novelists and the odd politician."

She looked at him, wide-eyed. "And you think they'll come to The Pretzel?"

"Yes," said Artie. "Some of them will. Now, has that shipment come in yet from the printer?"

"No, not yet. It should be here in a couple of hours. They've called twice, though, asking about payment."

"C.O.D. as agreed," said Artie. He opened his briefcase and counted out five one-hundred-dollar bills. "For the telegrams. They're a priority. But before you do that I want you to make one call for me. We have twenty thousand small leaflets that I would like dropped over the city twice daily between now and Friday afternoon. Try the trafficopter pilot at a local radio station. Obviously, his boss doesn't have to know that he's doing this for us. Offer him two hundred and fifty dollars. Settle for three hundred. Oh, and throw in an invitation to our grand opening Friday night. Okay?"

She looked at him in admiration. "Okay. I'll do my best."

* * *

On Wednesday morning the *Denver Post* contained

126

six strange little ads in various strategic sections of the paper. The ads were black with white writing and all read the same:

IF YOU'RE NOT AT THE PRETZEL
YOU'RE NOWHERE

There was a stark expanse of black for a full two-and-a-half inches of the four-inch ad, then a small white pretzel and under it:

The Pretzel
Opens July 27th
5000 Gregor Ave., Glendale, Colorado,
(303) 639-5000

At the bottom right-hand corner, almost imperceptible because of the ad's size, were the words: *Presented by A.*

During the afternoon rush hour thousands of handbills dropped mysteriously from the sky over downtown Denver. These were in the standard Pretzel format, only this time the slogan read:

HEAVEN-SENT

The Pretzel's staff of twelve was delighted with the publicity. It gave them a feeling of importance, with just a touch of conspiracy, and inspired them to work long past quitting time to finish the day's all-important tasks. At noon that day, Joe and his workers escorted Artie into the plant to survey the progress to date. The solvent smell of paint was pungent, but the entire room was now a rich, shiny

127

black, and the offending pieces of machinery had been moved against the walls. A dough mixer, a pretzel shaper and an oven had appeared at the head of the conveyor belt so that the entire pretzel-making process would be visible.

The men looked on anxiously as Artie surveyed the room. Finally he nodded and said, "I like it."

There was an audible sigh of relief and pleasure from the crew.

That afternoon Artie placed another telephone call to his hysterical counselors saying that he was okay but still tied up and would not be available until Saturday morning.

Ambulance group was holding up pretty well under the circumstances, except that Rob was losing his ability to function. The sleepless night and worried day were taking their toll on him and he had developed the involuntary habit of looking around corners, down alleys, up stairways and in doors in the hope that Artie might be there. Dennis was worried about Artie too, but refused to allow it to ruin his stay in Denver. If the boys were worried about anyone it was not Artie but Rob. They were attempting to distract and entertain him at all times, and were succeeding only in aggravating him further.

Rob's concerns were three-fold: first, a fear that Butcher would show up and take a head-count of Ambulance group; second, an anxiety that something might happen to Artie; third, a gut feeling that *nothing* would happen to Artie and that he would be successful in whatever he was doing, thus bringing calamity down on all their heads. The world had become a very hazy place for Rob. Only one thing was clear—had he elected to stay home and paint houses in suburban Montreal, he would definitely not have to worry about such things.

* * *

It was a slow day in the spectacular career of Malcolm Lloyd, star of stage, screen and television—the slowest he could remember since his starring role in the film *Confessions of a Closet Philatelist* had vaulted him to stardom. No one wanted to interview him or photograph his famous face; no one was offering him any new parts in any films; no one even wanted him to endorse a new shampoo. Nothing.

But what was this bizarre invitation he had just received? "*You are invited to The Pretzel,*" he read. "What's The Pretzel?" Interested, he reached for his phone.

* * *

"I'm sorry, Mr. Lloyd, but I can't connect you to the boss," said Miss Finch, her heart fluttering at the sound of his famous voice. "... No, Mr. Lloyd, he's not taking any calls ... No, I don't think he's going to be taking any calls later either. You see, he's very busy ... No, sir, I'm afraid I can't tell you who the boss is ... Oh, yes, sir, we know who you are ... Yes, sir, that I can say. We like to call it a disco with a twist ... Well, so many other people from the entertainment industry are invited that an actor of your stature certainly warrants an invitation ... Oh, I'm not at liberty to say, sir ... Well, Mr. Lloyd, if there's any further information you may need, please don't hesitate to call."

She hung up the phone and turned to Artie. "How did I do?"

"Fine," said Artie, with a slight smile. The wheels were in motion.

* * *

The first thing Malcolm Lloyd did after getting off the line with Miss Finch was to telephone a friend of his who worked at Channel Seven in Denver.

"What's all this about The Pretzel, Jerry? What is it?"

"Nobody's sure," was the reply. "We didn't hear of it until this morning when all those flyers and ads suddenly appeared. So now everybody knows *about* The Pretzel, but nobody knows what it is."

"The girl I talked to said it was some kind of disco," said Lloyd.

That was news to Jerry. The six o'clock report on Channel Seven aired a feature on The Pretzel, Denver's hottest and most mysterious disco, hinting broadly that many celebrities, including Hollywood's Malcolm Lloyd, could be expected to attend the opening on Friday. Their camera crew had actually attempted to get inside the factory, but burly Joe and several of his men had refused them admittance, under threat of physical violence if necessary.

By Thursday morning, the phones were ringing

130

the walls down in the office of The Pretzel. Artie steadfastly refused interviews, and had the desperate pleas for any information answered with, "We're a disco with a twist."

As more advertisements appeared around the city, more flyers fell from the sky, more reporting teams combed Denver for the slightest clue, and more famous personalities telephoned for information, Artie was supervising the establishment of a massive portable dance floor in the center of his disco. All eleven of his men formed a human barrier to keep out members of the press as the truck backed in the open bay doors of the factory. When it left, similar measures were taken.

Miss Finch was in a fever of excitement. She was speaking with celebrities from all walks of life and had to tell most of them, nicely and apologetically, that they could not be put through to her mysterious boss because he was "much too busy."

Late Thursday afternoon a large truck arrived at The Pretzel carrying what was claimed to be the loudest sound system in Denver. While Artie's crew was installing it, Artie instructed Miss Finch to phone around the city and rent every piece of lighting equipment available. "Rent it all," he advised. "Anything you can get your hands on. Lots of color, please, and plenty of flash. And mirrors. All the mirrors you can find. I've got to make some more arrangements. I'll be in again in a couple of hours. Is my tuxedo back from the cleaners?"

"Yes, it's in the closet in your office with the new shirt you asked for." She couldn't resist adding,

"Make sure you take out all the pins, dear."

* * *

That evening Joe, accompanied by Artie, paid visits to the four most popular bars in Denver's downtown hub. With Artie waiting in the car, Joe offered each of the four owners the opportunity to handle some of the drinks on Friday night at The Pretzel. Once he had adequately convinced them that he really was a representative of the now-legendary Pretzel, all agreed eagerly. The deal was that The Pretzel would have four bar stations, all privately owned and independent of each other. Each would have to bring his own bar and supplies (except for napkins, which Artie was having printed) and would pay The Pretzel twenty percent of all revenues. The Pretzel also reserved the right to set prices for all four bar stations; on Friday night a regular drink would tip the scale at seven dollars.

A similar arrangement was made with a small downtown restaurant called Tilly's, which would be serving food to the patrons of The Pretzel. This was to be kept simple, restricted to either an assorted cheese board or small trays of canapés.

Artie and Joe returned to the pretzel factory just in time to see a crew taking down the old sign and replacing it with a new one. Modeled after Artie's ad campaign the sign featured a black background with an enormous white neon pretzel, under which appeared the relatively small words *The Pretzel*.

Artie entered the factory, walked through the bustling main room and opened the door to the office. Miss Finch was shouting into the telephone, "I don't care *how* you get it just so long as you get it! This is for The Pretzel, so get a move on!" She hit a button, silencing another ringing phone. "Pretzel—how may I help you? . . . Ah, yes . . . "

* * *

On the third page of the *Denver Post* Friday morning, Artie's customary small ad had grown to take a quarter of the whole sheet. It contained the usual information, with the added note:

10:30 TONIGHT
PRIORITY TO INVITED GUESTS
ADMISSION NOT GUARANTEED

Denver was in a tizzy. All three TV stations had camera crews staked out at the airport to catch the movie stars and celebrities arriving on every flight. The Pretzel was on everyone's lips. The *Rocky Mountain News* called it "the most exciting event in the past twenty-five years." The *Post* predicted "a monstrous turnout" for opening night.

At one o'clock in the afternoon Artie was called in to inspect his disco. Everything was in place, and the bar and food stations were being assembled and stocked by their individual owners.

Joe could barely conceal his pride of accomplishment. "Well?"

Artie looked around critically. "I like it. A lot," he said finally.

The crew glowed.

133

Artie walked into the office area where two more of his men were setting up the DJ's booth. Spying her boss, Miss Finch got up and walked over to him, wringing her hands.

"Oh, Artie, we've all worked so hard for this! I'm so nervous, aren't you?"

Artie looked surprised. "No."

* * *

"This is a lost cause," announced Sam in disgust as the Ambulance cruised the streets of the city center for the umpteenth time. "We're never going to find him this way. I mean, I don't want to be anti-social, but I'm bored and tired and, no offense, Shel, but I don't want to hear any more about Pete Ogrodnick's sprained ankle. I don't even know the guy. Why don't we either decide to do something and do it or decide to do nothing and go to sleep?"

"We're doing something," said Rob with determination. "We're looking for Artie."

"You know, Nevin, Sam's right," said Dennis. "Besides, Artie said he'd be with us tomorrow. He's never let us down before."

"Spare me," said Rob. "Why would he have to stay today and not be able to leave until tomorrow? What's so important about today?"

"It's the day I went nuts sitting in a van," muttered Sam sourly.

"I don't think we looked hard enough for a planetarium," Howie complained.

"Well, at least one good thing came out of it," said Dennis. "I managed to grab this great flyer for my room. Free, too. I took it right off a fence." He held up the flyer for all to admire. "It's one of those Pretzel ads. Isn't it a beauty?" He sighed. "The grand opening's tonight. They've got all kinds of celebrities coming. I wish we could be there."

"Oh, sure," said Rob. "Go dance the night away. We haven't got a worry in the world."

Dennis was still staring at the flyer as though transfixed. "Imagine—being in Denver tonight and missing out on The Pretzel. It must be some slick operation. *Grand Opening Tonight. Presented by A. A?* Hmmm. That's strange. *A.* Oh—oh, Rob, you don't suppose . . . ?"

The screech of tires cut the air as Rob slammed on the brakes. "What? What did you say?"

"Well, I don't know exactly, but no one had ever heard of The Pretzel until we got to Denver, and the grand opening is tonight, and it's presented by *A,* and I don't know . . . it could never happen, but—"

"That Artie!" exclaimed Sam in admiration. "What a guy! And in our group, yet!"

"Artie is The Pretzel?" asked Kevin in disbelief.

"Let's go!" shouted Rob, pulling into a lane and turning the van around.

"Where?"

"The Pretzel! We're going to crash a party!"

With Dennis navigating, Ambulance group headed for the suburb of Glendale and the world's most chic disco.

From three blocks down the street the great neon pretzel shone out of the darkness, looking as though it hung unsupported in the air, a disoriented electric eel chasing its tail.

In anticipation of great traffic problems, the city of Denver had sent two traffic officers to keep things moving. Taxis, private cars and rented limousines were everywhere, and the small factory parking lot filled up almost immediately. Dennis and Rob were waved past and had to settle for a parking spot half a mile away from The Pretzel. Even at that distance they could hear the music. They finally arrived at the mirrored door a little after eleven. There was an enormous line-up extending down the block and around the corner. If there was any doubt in Rob's mind that this was a brainchild of Artie Geller it was dispelled by the sign: *Cover Charge $20. No Coins, Please.*

At the entrance stood a doorman in a red uniform with gold braid and tassel. Behind him sat a large muscular man who was collecting money and overseeing the admission process. When Ambulance group got there the doorman was welcoming the glamorous Fifi Latour, star of TV's hit comedy series, *Mademoiselle Schwartz*. She was escorted by astronaut Troy Stratos, who was famous not so much for the dubious distinction of having been the forty-third man to orbit Earth as for his renown as an international playboy.

Rob tried to walk in the door but the seated man, Joe, put an iron grip on his arm. The doorman fixed Rob with a long-nosed stare and snorted with disdain. He said, "How kind of you, sir, to save me the trouble of admitting all these other fine people before the obvious pleasure of admitting you. Truly noble, but I fear I must decline. Please go to the end of the line. You can't miss it. You merely follow this queue of people until there aren't any more, and then you stand there."

"But you don't understand," said Rob. "I've got to see Artie Geller."

The seated man stood up. "What business have you got with the boss?" he asked gruffly.

"He's one of the Ambulance group," piped Sam.

"Just tell him that Dennis and Rob are here to see him," said Dennis.

The big man beckoned a replacement over and disappeared inside the building for a few minutes. When he returned he was looking more kindly. "All right, you and your party follow me."

The step through the door from the outside world into The Pretzel was a step into another dimension. The music was deafening, its heavy beat and bass notes jarring the senses, its wailing highs assaulting the mind. The Pretzel was not merely a room: it was light and color at their acrobatic best. Hundreds of lights mounted on the ceiling, walls and even on the dance floor flashed, blazed, waved and shimmered, and the mirrors played them back a hundredfold.

The disco was already mobbed. Rob could not help wondering what it would be like when the people in line outside were all admitted. The dance floor was thick with gyrating bodies moving in harmony with the lights and sound. All the chairs and tables were occupied, and the bar stations and food center were operating at capacity. In one corner two bakers were filling a machine with salted dough, and a few yards away an enormous crowd of people joyously snatched hot pretzels from a conveyor belt.

The air was heavy with smoke and the smell of freshly baked dough.

Ambulance group was led out of the disco and into a suite of offices. There, behind a large polished mahogany desk, reclining in a padded swivel chair and munching contentedly on a hot pretzel, sat Artie in full business regalia.

Rob saw red. "Artie, what *is* this?"

Howie nudged him. "Pssst, Rob—it's a disco."

"I know it's a disco! What I want to know is where that little crook gets the *nerve,* the sheer, unadulterated nerve to—"

The big man who had brought them in turned on Rob. "Hey, you! Show some respect! Don't you know who you're talking to?"

"Yes, I know *exactly* who I'm talking to! I'm talking to Artie Geller, an eleven-year-old runaway from Juniortours! That's who I'm talking to!"

Miss Finch looked at Artie. "Is this true?"

Artie shrugged.

A man appeared in the doorway. "Artie, our count's at eighteen hundred, but I think we can fit a lot more in."

"Go to it," said Artie. The man disappeared.

"Wow!" breathed Kevin. "Eighteen hundred people times the twenty-dollar admission—that's thirty-six thousand dollars!"

"Is it?" said Artie mildly. "I never was much at math."

Dennis spoke up. "Well, look, Artie, we think it's a wonderful place you have here, and we're proud of you for doing all this. But we really have to—" His voice trailed off as a strange-looking man dressed entirely in metallic blue danced his way into the office. "Oh!" gasped Dennis. "You're—you're—" he snapped his fingers. "Mike Banshee, the lead singer of Sheep Dip!"

"Yeah, man. I just wanted to tell the little boss here that this is a truly cosmic place he's running." He turned to Artie. "My man, this place has vibes! It's, like, the Fourth of July-H-bomb-reality-kalei-doscope-*big!* It *is, was* and *will be,* man! And I say that with all mega-sincerity!"

Artie smiled politely. "I'm glad you're having a good time, Mr. Banshee."

"Oh, can I have your autograph?" Dennis begged. "I have all your albums!"

The apparation in blue scribbled something on a piece of paper from Artie's desk and danced back to the disco.

"All right, Artie," said Rob. "Let's get going."

Dennis looked at Rob as though he were completely insane. "We can't leave—this is the chance of a lifetime! There are important people out there!"

"You'll be staying, of course," said Artie.

"Oh, can we?" The five boys charged up to Artie's desk and began slapping him on the back in a great show of brotherhood.

"We can't stay," argued Rob. "We can't afford to sniff the air out there."

"*My* people," said Artie, "don't pay." He scribbled a note on a piece of paper and handed it to Dennis. "This is good for anything you need. Have a good time."

Dennis was beside himself with pleasure. "Artie, you're a prince!"

"Aren't you going to come with us?" asked Sheldon.

"Oh, no," said Artie. "I'm working."

A staff member walked in and placed a carton full of money on the desk. "Plenty more where that came from, boss."

Artie reached for his calculator.

"Come on, Rob," called Dennis. "The whole world's out there."

Rob looked tempted. "Artie, I want your word that as soon as this is over we all drive to New Mexico. If we go all night we can make it and be only a few hours late."

Artie nodded. "You have my word."

A little difference of opinion

Roll 11, exposures 1-36. The Pretzel.

Artie had neglected to mention that closing time for
The Pretzel was four in the morning and that it
would take forty minutes to clear the building of
the almost twenty-eight hundred guests who had
come to the grand opening. Many of the celebrity
guests had stayed behind to thank and congratulate
their host. Artie had sent out two hundred and fifty
VIP invitations, and more than a hundred of the
famous personalities had actually attended—a sur-
prisingly good percentage.

It took another two hours to settle with the bar
and food people and to pay his staff their remaining
salary, plus large bonuses for their dedication. He
even included in their pay envelopes letters of rec-
ommendation to their next employers. These were
signed *A, The Pretzel, Denver.*

It was an emotional farewell scene between Artie
and his faithful staff. Miss Finch sobbed uncontrol-

lably, and even big Joe looked a little misty-eyed. Sheldon too was obviously deeply affected, the scene calling up memories of the departure of Pete Ogrodnick, so he began to sniffle as well. Artie shook hands with all of them and headed for the door. He turned, surveyed the room critically, said, "I like it," and was gone.

Ambulance group drove straight to Interstate 25, heading for Albuquerque or bust. Dennis, who was at the wheel, had promised a super-express, non-stop trip, hopefully making Albuquerque in seven and a half hours. The group was strangely silent for the first half hour, then Rob turned around in his seat and glared at Artie threateningly.

"You know, if I hadn't had the greatest time in my life last night I'd be in the process of killing you right now."

"I'm glad you enjoyed it," said Artie mildly.

"But when Butcher blows his stack at us for being late I'm going to give you to him, Artie, on a silver platter. How does that grab you?"

Artie said nothing.

"That was one beautiful disco you put together, Artie," Dennis called back. "Thanks for showing us such a good time."

All at once conversation swelled in the back seat.

"I met a real basketball star! He was seven-foot-four!"

"I saw two astronauts! *Two!*"

"Kevin won the Seven-Up races!"

"Kevin threw up in the washroom!"

"Did you see Rob dancing with Belinda Egan?"

Rob smiled. Young Belinda, star of such films as

A Parisian in Cripple Creek and *Sequined Sneakers,* had been the highlight of his evening. His status as a personal guest of *A* had brought him up to her level.

"Artie, how did you do it?"

Artie shrugged. "Oh, a little of this and that."

"Yeah, well, a little of this and that certainly made you a few bucks," said Rob. "You're not going to tell me that those two big cartons of money contain 'nothing much.' And those aren't just ones in there. They're tens and twenties and fifties. I'm starting to get nervous around you and your treasury. We shouldn't be in a van—we should be driving a Brinks truck."

Artie's accounting of the situation was still crude at this point. The cost of the disco had drained his resources, leaving him within two hundred dollars of bankruptcy, but The Pretzel had brought him approximately sixty thousand dollars. His briefcase, then, held only his tuxedo, and his fortune lay in the two corrugated cardboard boxes on which he rested his feet. A bank in Albuquerque would have the privilege of converting it into an array of bills that would fit into the case.

* * *

In blistering heat the Ambulance pulled into the campground late Saturday afternoon. Following Rob's plan the group disembarked and immediately set about establishing the lived-in look about their campsite. Butcher apprehended them in the act. He drove up, screeched to a halt and lumbered over.

Rage, fury and disbelief wafted across his contorted features in shades of red and purple. Dennis and Rob prepared themselves for an onslaught of yelling hitherto undreamt of.

"Gee," announced Howie loudly, "we sure have been at this trailer camp a *long* time."

"All right, I'm going to remain calm, cool and collected while you two Canadian Ambulance guys tell me where you've been."

"We were in Denver," Dennis said weakly. "It really is a—uh—a fascinating city. Makes you forget the time."

"Don't give me that!" growled Butcher. "I want to know why you're late and I want to know *now!*"

This is it, thought Rob—the moment of truth. He would denounce Artie as the culprit and tell Butcher everything—The Pretzel, the milk store, the Capitol Hill speedway and attack jelly. This time Butcher would have to listen and Artie would be sent home as he deserved. Yes, Rob decided, he would do this for the good of everybody. He was about to do it. In just a few seconds he *would* do it. The words were all ready.

He opened his mouth. "Mr. Butcher, the fact is that we liked Denver, the kids liked Denver and we stayed a bit late."

"And we caught up with the tour," Dennis added, "so no one'll ever know the difference."

"Yes, someone'll know the difference! Try the Colorado State Police and the New Mexico State Police! They know the difference already—they're looking for you right now! What have you got to say to that?"

"Better tell them you found us," said Sam.

With much effort Butcher forced the corners of his mouth up in an absurd smile. "Sorry, guys, this is between your counselors and me." He turned back to Dennis and Rob. "In America, when you're on a tour you follow a schedule. When you go wherever you feel like going it's not a tour anymore! Got it?"

They nodded dumbly.

"Now, I've never fired a counselor before, but if I hear one more tiny little peep out of this group—the slightest little mishap—if you're half an hour late, *you're gone!*"

They nodded again.

"I want you to know right now that my report on you is going to say that you're the two most irresponsible people I ever met in my life!" He stalked off, jumped into his car and pulled away. As the roar of the engine grew fainter a new sound reached their ears—the steady laughter of Byron of the Road Hogs. Dennis shot him a nasty look and he walked away, still laughing.

Rob suggested a nap for what remained of the afternoon, but the day was hot and uncomfortable and a dip in the pool seemed a more popular idea. Only Artie opted for the nap, though his purpose, probably, was to remain close to his two cartons of money.

Rob went with the others to the pool but did not change into his swimsuit, preferring to lounge in a deck chair and try to doze off. Sleep, however, would not come. He found his mind wandering to the latest run-in with Butcher and his own failure to put the blame on Artie. The Road Hogs were at the pool too, he noticed without interest.

Dennis sent Sheldon to the van for some extra towels. The boy disappeared for a moment, then came running back with an armful, jogging past a group of Road Hog campers. Nonchalantly one of them stuck out a foot. Sheldon tripped and fell heavily to the ground.

"Hey!" Sam rose out of the water like a Polaris missile. He singled out the offender and dealt him a punch to the face and then one to the chest. The other Road Hogs grabbed him, but he shook his arms free.

"Mark, are you all right?" Byron and Darryl jogged onto the scene and Darryl grabbed Sam by the shoulders. "Hey, Ambulance!" he called. "Your little twit's getting too big for his pants! Here, take him!" He shoved Sam away, sending him sprawling to the concrete apron of the pool.

"Why, you miserable—!" His face flaming bright red, Dennis scrambled out of the water and headed for the Road Hogs with murder in his eye.

Rob who had been attending to Sam, ran up and grabbed his partner less than a yard away from Darryl. "Dennis, control yourself! We don't want any trouble here!"

"'We don't want any trouble here,'" mimicked Byron in a mocking falsetto.

Dennis struggled hard to break free of Rob. "If you want to hit someone to make yourself feel like a big man, you can hit me! But you hit one of my kids—now you're going to die for it!"

"Big talk!" Darryl sneered.

146

"Where's your little weirdo?" Byron added.

Rob turned his attention from Dennis. "Our *what?*"

"That weird little kid you've got—the wimpy one who carries the briefcase." Byron saw the look on Rob's face and dug harder. "You know, the *freak.*"

There was a moment of total silence. Then Rob, the peacemaker, let go of Dennis, took a powerful step forward and swung mightily.

* * *

Artie woke up from a light sleep to hear the chatter of his Ambulance-mates coming back from the pool. In through the tent flap staggered seven valiant fighters, battle-scarred with bruises and assorted scrapes and cuts.

"What happened?" Artie asked.

Dennis grinned through rapidly swelling lips. "A little difference of opinion with the Road Hogs."

"We showed them we've got guts!" yelled Sam, waving a fist.

"That's because they were scattering them all over the pool," gasped Rob, rubbing his jaw.

"Did we win?" asked Sheldon.

"Morally, yes," said Dennis.

"What does that mean?" asked Howie, examining a scraped knee.

"It means we got pummeled," said Rob. "Dennis, get the first-aid kit. I hope there's enough iodine to go around."

"They killed us," mourned Kevin.

"Hah!" said Sam. "They looked pretty beat-up too."

"Their fists will be sore anyway," said Rob, dabbing at Nick's elbow with a handkerchief.

"It's too bad you weren't there, Artie," said Sam. "That would have evened things up. We were outnumbered."

"Did they attack you?" asked Artie in concern.

"Oh, no," said Dennis. "They were being a pain in the neck as usual, insulting our group, so Rob hit one of them."

"That was his first good decision," said Sam positively. "What a punch! Knocked him right into the pool!"

"I was proud of you, Nevin," said Dennis, "sticking up for the guys like that. It was beautiful!"

"It was stupid. I darn near got us all killed."

"It was great! You knocked Byron clear into the next county!"

"And all this time I thought the uglier one was Darryl," said Rob. "Pass the bandages, please. Sheldon, does that hurt?"

"Yes."

"And this was the Road Hogs?" asked Artie. "Those big guys in that brown van?"

"The very same," said Rob.

"Well, maybe we didn't win technically," said Sam, "but we sure proved that they can be hit."

"We also proved that they can hit back," said Rob. "Dennis, you'll need some ice on that."

"We were winners in the end," Dennis insisted. "We came out of it with self-respect."

"Well, I sure hope we've got enough self-respect to last the rest of the tour," said Rob. "I don't think I could go through *that* again."

"Okay, team," said Dennis cheerfully, his words somewhat slurred from the swelling of his mouth, "we upheld our honor on the field of battle, and now it's on to our next adventure, the Grand Canyon."

"I hope the Road Hogs fall in," said Sheldon.

"But they provoked you, right?" said Artie with interest.

"Oh, yeah," said Sam. "They were looking for a fight and we gave it to them."

"And they gave it right back to us," said Rob. "And if we don't arrive at the Grand Canyon on time we're going to get it from another unpleasant source. Whoa—Artie, just what do you think you're doing?"

"Nothing," said Artie, stepping into his tuxedo pants.

"Don't give me that," said Rob. "Every time you put that monkey suit on you disappear somewhere, and suddenly, halfway across town, a thriving business whooshes into being. Where are you going?"

"No place."

"Artie, I'm not stupid!"

Artie crawled out of the tent and stood for a moment, brushing off his tuxedo and drawing on his immaculate white gloves. "I'm not leaving the camp," he promised. "I won't be more than about twenty minutes. Wait here for me." He marched off.

Dennis, Rob and the five campers scrambled out

149

of the tent and anxiously watched Artie's progress across the compound.

"Oh, my God!" breathed Rob. "He's going to the Road Hogs!"

"Oh, no!" cried Dennis. "What does he think he can do to them? They'll kill kim!"

"Okay!" Sam exclaimed, slamming his fist into his palm. "Let's get over there and back him up."

"Don't anybody move!" commanded Rob. "If Artie needs rescuing, Dennis and I will do it."

The group watched in trepidation as Artie tapped on the Road Hogs' tent flap and entered. Total silence fell. Even Sheldon had no parallel experience in the life of Pete Ogrodnick to relate. The seven stood frozen, eyes riveted on the Road Hogs' tent.

Fifteen minutes passed and Dennis could stand it no longer. "Nevin, we've got to do something! That's our kid in there! Who knows what they're doing to him?"

Rob frowned. "I figured he'd come sailing out after five seconds. What are they doing in there?"

Finally the tent flap lifted, and Byron and Darryl both hurried out. Byron held the flap open for Artie, who emerged dapper as ever. Smiling broadly, the two Road Hogs shook hands with the boy. Darryl straightened Artie's tie, patted him affectionately on the shoulder and Artie started back across the compound. Spying Ambulance group watching spellbound, Byron waved in a friendly way, calling, "Hey, guys, see you at the Grand Canyon."

Mouth open, Dennis waved back feebly.

Rob reached out and grasped the returning Artie by his satin lapels. "Are you all right?"

"Sure."

Dennis turned wide eyes on his charge. "What happened in there?"

"Nothing."

* * *

It was Rob's turn to drive, and the group left forty-five minutes early, just to be on the safe side.

The topic of conversation in the van was Artie's visit to the Road Hogs. Artie, who had converted his bulky fortune to large bills before leaving Albuquerque, took on his usual pose, sitting with his attaché case in his lap, dodging and avoiding all direct questions as to exactly what had taken place in the Road Hogs' tent.

"I still can't believe it," Rob was saying. "I figured they were going to send you back in a shoe box. Now they're being nice and polite and friendly—come on, Artie. Just this once, tell us what you did."

"Nothing—we just had a discussion."

"You didn't pay them off, did you?"

"Of course not."

"He couldn't have," added Nick. "His money was still in the Ambulance."

"Well, then, you threatened them," Rob persisted.

Artie shrugged. "How could I?"

At Thoreau, Arizona, they crossed the continental divide. Kevin, whose artistic mind had been imagining great rivers separating east and west, had to content himself with a few snapshots of the wind-blown sign which read, *You are now crossing the Great Divide,* to which someone had added in purple lipstick, *Big deal!*

"It's lousy," announced Sam, and there was total agreement.

"The tour book calls it a geological wonder," said Rob.

"Yeah," snorted Dennis. "I wonder where it is. Let's get going."

To Rob's great relief they arrived at the Grand Canyon in mid-evening. They were greeted at the campground by the Road Hogs, who had made popcorn and insisted on sharing. Ambulance group provided the toast.

* * *

Rolls 12-14, exposures 1-36. The Grand Canyon.

The Grand Canyon was everything Kevin and camera could want. Armed with three rolls of film and various lenses, he set out to capture all aspects of one of the world's great spectacles.

Sam was disgusted when he was informed that he was not old enough to venture into the Canyon on mule-back. Since his original desire had been to shoot the rapids of the Colorado River, he felt that being denied the mule trip—his second choice—was the ultimate indignity.

"I can't believe this!" he muttered after his attempt to pass himself off as thirteen had been repulsed by an annoyed tour guide. "It just goes to show you—you drive far enough away from the Statue of Liberty and they forget what it means! What is this? You're not a person until you're twelve?"

Sheldon was happy for the same reason that Sam was miserable. He had accepted Sam's triple dare to take the mule trip and had intended to go through with it even if it killed him, which he was certain it would. Now he looked at his surroundings with the eyes of a man given a new lease on life.

Dennis was sure he was in paradise, for every three steps brought him to another Indian artifact to buy. On his head he wore the full-feathered headdress from Ohio, and to this he added a Hopi Indian blanket which he hung from his belt, and Indian moccasins. His hands were covered with native rings, and he carried a bag which contained an assortment of Grand Canyon pennants, paperweights, ashtrays, posters and other paraphernalia.

"Dennis, where are you getting all that money?" Rob asked suspiciously as Dennis pulled out a twenty-dollar bill and began to gaze intently at a miniature totem pole. "You've been busted since Columbus."

Dennis flushed. "I've been meaning to tell you, Rob, because some of this is yours. Artie paid me back all the money we spent on him when we thought he was broke."

"Oh, yeah? I didn't know we loaned him that much."

"Well—we didn't. He also gave us sort of a bonus."

Rob was appalled. "That's corruption! It's hush money! It's a pay-off so we won't tell what he's been up to! And you took it?"

"Well, we did kind of help him out with the cows and—"

"Give me that!" Rob snatched the bill out of Dennis's hand. "It goes right back to Artie. It's dirty money and we don't want anything to do with it!"

"Aw, Rob—"

"I wonder what Butcher would say it he found out one of his counselors is on the take. Dennis, you're a worm!"

The group returned to camp for dinner to find the Ambulance gleaming white and Byron and Darryl putting the finishing touches on the chrome with polishing cloths.

"We were washing our van, and since you're parked right next to us we figured we'd do yours too," explained Darryl. "It's nothing, really. It didn't take long."

"Uh—thanks, guys," said Dennis weakly. "Thanks a lot."

After supper all the groups stopped by the Canyon for a final look before moving on. Dozens of counselors and campers strolled over to the rim to gaze out at the breathtaking panorama.

Rob was pondering the millions of years of Earth's history laid out before him. But the secrets that lay hidden in those rock strata were as insignificant as the trail of a worm through dry sand when compared with the secret of what Artie had said or done to the Road Hogs that afternoon in Albuquerque. And, he thought with a shudder, if the Road Hogs didn't frighten Artie, how could he and Dennis ever expect to control him?

* * *

Agent Frank Newman of the FBI was seated at his desk pondering a recent diamond smuggling case when his assistant, Agent Tim O'Reilly, burst into the room.

"Frank, I think I've got something."

Newman sat forward in his chair. "Good. These smugglers are really starting to get me down."

"Not that. I'm talking about the kid-in-the-tuxedo thing."

"Oh." In Newman's opinion that case was the least important of their assignments. "All right, what is it?"

"Remember that big disco in Denver Friday night? That was another one, complete with the little kid in the tuxedo and everything. He called himself A."

"Yeah, but wasn't The Pretzel a legitimate operation?"

O'Reilly shook his head. "No licenses, no permits—and the morning after, no Pretzel. They shut the whole thing down and flew the coop. Not only that, but the building they used belongs to Twister Pretzel, and they don't know anything about the disco. Anyway, we guessed the probable routes between Washington and Denver and came up with an incident at this big state park in Nebraska—something called a 'no-frills milk store.' Some kid in a tuxedo was charging people a buck a minute to milk a cow."

Newman whistled. "And people were paying it?"

"Honestly, Frank, the public doesn't deserve our protection. But anyway, he rented the cows from this nearby farmer and, like before—no license, no permit, no nothing—he ran the place for three days, made about four grand and took off." O'Reilly spread out a map on the desk. "Now, we've marked all the spots he's hit. There's the attack jelly in New York, that gambling thing on Capital Hill, the milk thing in Nebraska, and The Pretzel in Denver."

Newman looked at the map. "Looks like one of those 'See America' tours."

"That's what I thought," said O'Reilly. "And there's one tour taking that exact route and hitting on the right days—Juniortours."

Newman frowned. "I've heard of them. But that's kids."

"Right. And we're looking for a little kid in a tuxedo."

A slow smile appeared on Newman's face. "I get it. Some crook figured that kids would never fall under suspicion, so he's using Juniortours kids to work his scams for him. Must be some weird guy, considering the kinds of schemes he's pulling off. But Juniortours fields lots of groups. How do we know which one will lead us to our man?"

O'Reilly grinned. "Well, Juniortours reported a van missing right after the tour left Denver and The Pretzel opened. It's probably the one we want. I've got a description from the New Mexico State Police. They're Group Ambulance or something like that."

Newman looked pleased. "Nice work. What's the tour's schedule right now?"

"According to the itinerary they're coming from the Grand Canyon, and they'll be in Vegas for the next couple of days."

Newman stood up. "Okay, we're going to Vegas."

* * *

The campers had all fallen asleep but the white van, with Rob at the wheel, still headed west on Interstate 14.

"You know, it's funny," Rob was saying, "when I was eleven and I got beat up, my eighteen-year-old brother would come and bail me out. Now I'm eighteen and an eleven-year-old is working things out for me. I'd give anything to know how he did it."

"I told you, Nevin," Dennis yawned. "They're a great bunch of kids!"

Rob shook his head. "I can't believe Artie. He's awful and yet—he has so much *style*."

"Well, I'm glad to see you've finally decided to like Artie."

"Wait a minute," Rob protested. "I never said I liked him. I mean, I like him . . . " He paused. "With reservations."

A sign loomed up on the right. *Welcome to Nevada, The Silver State.* Suddenly, Rob slammed on the brakes and the van screeched to a stop in the last few yards of New Mexico.

"What's going on?" asked Dennis.

Rob pointed to the sign identifying the state line.

"So? We're entering Nevada."

"We're entering Nevada *with Artie!*" Rob corrected. "This is the money state, Dennis! We can't take that kid to Las Vegas! The whole city is pure money!"

Dennis looked disgusted. "Nevin, I thought you said you trusted Artie."

"I said I liked him with reservations, and this is one of the reservations. We'll go around Nevada."

"Don't be an idiot. If we don't check in at Las Vegas we're both fired. Now get moving! You don't stop dead in the middle of an Interstate! And just leave Artie to me. He can't gamble under the age of twenty-one anyway."

Reluctantly Rob started up again. "Hmmmph! When a fifty-storey ivory tower appears in downtown Las Vegas, with a disco on the top floor, a milk store in the basement and a racetrack out back, and suddenly there's an attack jelly mailorder service, don't say I didn't warn you!"

"Nevin, you worry too much."

Adventures of the old guy

In the campsite just outside the Las Vegas city limits Ambulance group slept the sleep of the exhausted. Missing entirely the activities of the morning, they woke up in time for lunch at noon, truly rested and refreshed for the first time since Denver.

They began the afternoon with a trip to Hoover Dam, taking the tour of the power plant, watching all the films and looking at all the exhibits. Here Howie showed the first sign of having an interest in anything that was unrelated to space. He seemed to have a keen fascination with the place and had to be restrained from asking questions during the recorded lectures.

Sheldon found that engineering details reminded him of Pete Ogrodnick. "I never understood this kind of stuff. Pete always understood it. Pete could listen to it for hours. I'll never forget the time we went to this nuclear power station ... "

Nick liked the ice cream more than anything else; Kevin liked the view, snapping endless pictures;

Sam was bored. Artie disappeared.

Rob was more disgusted than shocked: his greatest fear had come to pass in no time at all. Artie was loose on Las Vegas.

"We'll just have to carry on as if this hadn't happened," Dennis decided. "We'll go on to Lake Mead just like we planned."

"Can we fish?" asked Sam.

"Sure thing. Okay, guys, let's move out."

* * *

At half past four the front door of the Lemay Theatrical Costume and Make-Up Studio opened and a little old man hobbled out, leaning heavily on a wooden cane. He had a shock of white hair and a thick mustache. His skin was wrinkled with age and he had a red-veined nose that was a little too large for his face. He wore a familiar tuxedo, with white gloves on his hands, and from underneath his bushy brows peered the lively dark eyes of Artie Geller. An eleven-year-old would not be allowed in the casinos, but an elderly gentleman would be most welcome.

He had an early dinner at a restaurant which advertised a fifteen percent discount for senior citizens, then he headed for a casino on the Strip.

Wordlessly Artie opened his briefcase and pushed ten thousand dollars across the counter to the cashier. She counted it carefully and then gave him a holder full of the casino's color-coded chips. "Ten thousand dollars, sir. Good luck."

He acknowledged her good wishes with a brief nod, hobbled over to a blackjack table and hoisted

160

himself onto an empty stool. There, still using sign language only, he began to play. The table limit was two thousand, and Artie opened with a bet of five hundred dollars. He drew 18; the dealer drew 20. Artie remained calm as his stakes were swept away. The next two rounds he went over 21, losing again. Then he began to win. His photographic memory catalogued the cards already played and he was able to predict what cards remained and the probability of his getting them. He increased his bets to a thousand dollars and then to the limit, two thousand, losing occasionally but in the end winning the majority of the hands. A mountain of chips began to grow in front of him.

Word quickly circulated in the casino that there was an old man on a streak at a blackjack table, and a crowd of spectators began to gather to watch him break the bank.

One of the observers was the Juniortours tour director himself, Charlie Butcher, who felt the Las Vegas leg of the trip was the only consolation for his job. He loved to gamble and blackjack was his game, although, for him, just breaking even was a triumph. He watched in admiration as the old man avoided any attempts to break his concentration, turning down complimentary drinks and never flinching as the dealer constantly changed the decks. Boy, thought Butcher, he could really learn from an old master like this!

Artie's winning streak continued until the assistant manager arrived to inform him politely that he could no longer play. "Feel free to avail yourself of any of our other facilities," he said, "but I'm afraid our blackjack tables are off limits to you. Congratulations on your big win."

There was some booing from the small crowd, but they were all familiar with house policy. Artie nodded understandingly, flipped the dealer a hundred-dollar chip as a tip, gathered his winnings and headed for the cashier. Butcher followed, noting with some perplexity that the old man looked strangely familiar.

As Artie was stuffing his new money into the attaché case Butcher approached him. "Say, old timer, that's quite a respectable game of blackjack you played there."

Artie smiled.

"Too bad they closed you out. Where are you headed next?"

Artie shrugged as if to say, "No place."

"Mind if I tag along?"

Artie shrugged again, and the two started out of the casino.

The assistant manager called over a plainclothes security man. "I want you to follow the old guy wherever he goes tonight and make sure nothing happens to him. Be bad for our image if he got rolled after winning here. See that guy who's with him? I don't trust fast friends of big winners. Got it?"

"Right, boss."

The selection process for the next casino was simple. Artie, with Butcher in tow and the security man tagging along at a discreet distance, merely marched into the casino of the next hotel down the Strip. He changed another ten thousand into chips and settled down at the blackjack table. Butcher converted all his ready cash—about two hundred dollars—into chips and took a seat beside Artie. Trying to match Artie's aggressive play, he made several bad decisions, and his money was gone in half an hour. By that time Artie was well on his way to shaping another sizeable win. Quite a crowd had gathered to cheer him on, but they did so quietly, careful not to break his concentration.

"Great move, Pops!"

"Don't let 'em psych you!"

That the house was aware of Artie became obvious when free drinks began arriving. Artie accepted these graciously and passed them on to Butcher, who, disgusted with his own game, was sucking them back as fast as they came.

The casino manager, watching Artie through the one-way mirror in his office, remarked to an aide, "This is a sharpie. Ease the old coot out of here. And send one of the boys to tail him—we can't have him getting mugged after a big win here."

So Artie was once more on his way, followed by a slightly tipsy Charlie Butcher and, about ten yards back, two security guards who turned out to be acquaintances from their old days at Wells-Fargo.

* * *

"All right, guys, what are we going to do tonight?" said Dennis after supper at the Las Vegas campsite.

"Stay here and wait for Artie," said Rob firmly.

"It figures you'd say something like that, Nevin," said Dennis in disgust. "We don't know when Artie's coming back and I'm not wasting an evening sitting here. Let's see the bright lights of the city, absorb the spectacle of Vegas. We'll go to Circus, Circus."

"But that's a casino!" Rob protested.

"There's an observation level where you don't gamble. We'll love it—right, guys?"

The campers were eager to be off and at quarter to nine the white van pulled out of the trailer park and headed for the city lights.

Twenty minutes later a royal blue Plymouth sedan pulled up at the front gate and two men dressed in dark clothing approached the park office. One flashed identification at the clerk on duty.

"Newman, FBI. We're looking for a white Juniortours van called Ambulance. Know it?"

"Oh, it's berthed here, all right," the woman replied, "but you won't find them. They went out a few minutes ago. They were headed into town."

"Thanks." Newman and O'Reilly got back into the car, made a wide illegal U-turn and drove off towards the city.

* * *

"I have a hard life," Butcher was saying, his words considerably slurred. He stood behind Artie, who was seated at his fifth blackjack table of the night. Four security guards from previous casinos hovered around the place, keeping an eye on the old man as per their instructions. "I work with Juniortours." He shuddered. "It's terrible. All those kids and teenage counselors. Yuck! You wouldn't believe what those guys do."

Artie clucked sympathetically, then raked in some chips as the dealer went over 21.

"That's not the worst of my troubles," Butcher rambled on. "There's these guys from Canada—the Am-Am-Ambulance group. Flakes, all of them. I tell you, if I didn't get to Vegas a couple of times a year I'd go crazy."

From his reverie Butcher heard what had become his favorite sentence as a waiter appeared, placed a drink down beside Artie and announced, "Compliments of the house, sir." Clumsily Butcher grabbed the glass and took a large gulp.

As Artie continued winning the familiar signs began to appear, leading to the inevitable ousting. He converted his chips into cash, made sure that Butcher hadn't wandered away—by now he felt a certain responsibility towards the man—and ventured outside. Yet a fifth man was dispatched to join the existing bodyguards, who performed the necessary introductions and shook hands all around. It was not often that the security personnel from so many different casinos got to meet socially.

* * *

Roll 15, exposure 14. The show at Circus, Circus. Note Rob in foreground, looking nervous.

Circus, Circus was spectacular, and Dennis, Rob and the five campers were enjoying it immensely. Of the seven, Rob had the most reservations. He felt he should be looking for Artie or, at the very least, be back at camp waiting for him.

Nearby, one man was raving to his companion, "You don't know what's been going on in this town. There's this little old man in a tuxedo—he looks seventy-five, maybe eighty—he's working the black-jack tables on the Strip and he's cleaning up. All the casinos are asking him to leave, so he just puts the money in this attaché case and moves on down the road."

The words "little," "tuxedo," "attaché case" and "cleaning up" broke through to Rob. His mind raced. It had to be Artie, it just had to be. Any little man wearing a tuxedo, carrying an attaché case with a lot of money and on the way to a lot more had to be Artie. The part about it being an old man was confusing, but it might be a disguise to get him into the casinos. In any case, they had to find him. He sidled up to Dennis and explained the situation.

Dennis seemed proud. "What a fiery little guy! Nothing can stop him!"

"This is serious, Dennis. He could get into a lot of trouble. We've got to get to him."

Grudgingly Dennis agreed. "I'll go tell the guys."

"You do that," said Rob. "And pray Butcher doesn't find out about this."

* * *

The white van cruised the Las Vegas Strip. "Here's the plan," said Rob. "We go to the hotels one at a time, run in and have a look around, and sooner or later we'll find him."

"But if he's disguised as this old man," said Dennis, "will we recognize him?"

"Don't be thick, Dennis. Of course we will. Same briefcase, same tuxedo—and anywhere there's a big crowd, there's probably Artie. Also, we know he's playing blackjack. Let's start with the Hilton."

166

They pulled into the parking lot and Dennis turned to the campers. "We'll just be a couple of minutes, guys. Wait for us in the van." The two jogged into the hotel entrance and, a few minutes later, jogged out again.

"Not in there," puffed Rob. "Let's move down one."

Dennis pulled into traffic and quickly turned back down the next driveway. He and Rob ran into the brilliantly-lit hotel. Two minutes later they were back.

"All right," said Rob with grim determination. "Next. We're going to find him if we have to check out every gambling place in Vegas!"

* * *

The royal blue Plymouth cruised the city, Agents Newman and O'Reilly scanning the roads and parking lots for the white van, Ambulance. O'Reilly was talking on the car's built-in phone. "Right... Thanks. We'll check it out. Frank, the local police say there've been sightings of that white van in and around the Strip."

"Okay," said Newman, "let's get over there."

* * *

Eight security men lounged comfortably about the casino of the Las Vegas Hotel Gunhold, keeping an eye on their elderly charge as he systematically mounted up another fortune.

Artie was playing with his usual unflappable flair. Butcher, now three sheets to the wind, was relating his life story, interspersing comments about his terrible job, Canada and Ambulance group into the narrative. Between Butcher's monologue and Artie's expert play a large audience was held spellbound.

Through the wide doors of the casino jogged Dennis and Rob, scanning the glittering bustle of the room. Rob's eyes fell immediately on the crowd surrounding the blackjack table. He searched the faces until he came to the old man. It was amazing—some make-up artist had put sixty-five years on the kid, but it was still Artie. The eyes gave it away, Rob decided, those dark eyes that knew so much and said so little.

"Pssst!" whispered Dennis. "There he is. Can you believe that?"

Rob nodded grimly. "Let's go get him."

"Wait a minute," said Dennis. "Who's that with him? Hey, it looks like—"

"Butcher!" finished Rob. "Oh no! We can't go up there! If Butcher sees us, that's it!"

"What's Butcher doing with Artie anyway?"

"I don't know," moaned Rob, shaking his head. "I don't know anything anymore."

"We'll have to wait here," Dennis decided. "As soon as Artie gets far enough away from Butcher, we'll grab him."

"What about the others?" asked Rob anxiously. "We've got five other kids besides this beast."

"Don't worry about them. They're good kids. We told them to stay in the van, and they'll stay in the van."

* * *

"We can't just stay in the van," Sam was saying.

"They've been gone a long time. They could be in trouble. Maybe Artie's in trouble."

"What kind of trouble?" asked Sheldon meekly.

"Big trouble," said Nick.

"We've got to help out," said Sam decisively. "It's our duty as members of Ambulance group. Right?"

"Right!"

"Okay, we'll need to disguise ourselves so we won't be recognized."

"Why?" asked Kevin.

"Uh—well, Artie's in disguise, so it must be important."

"Right!"

"But we don't have any disguises," Howie pointed out.

"Hmmm, you're right," said Sam. "I guess we'll have to improvise. Now, let's see . . . "

Five minutes later the campers emerged from the van splendidly arrayed in Dennis's lovingly collected souvenirs. Sam wore the gigantic fringed sombrero; Kevin's face was all but lost in the Indian headdress; Nick almost completely disappeared inside the huge Indian blanket. Howie was selected to wear the dome of the Capitol building with the red, white and blue streamers. That left Sheldon without a costume, so he was chosen to carry the heavy artillery in case of emergency—Dennis's sixteen-pound block of pure steel. Sheldon also decided to wear his Cow Expert T-shirt, as he felt it would earn him the respect of those around him. On his head was a Chicago Cubs baseball hat, which seemed to Sam to be slightly traitorous but, after all, this was an emergency.

Since the souvenirs had been bought to fit Dennis, the headgear restricted the campers' vision considerably, and it was only with much bumping into each other that the boys deployed themselves. They staggered and stumbled in through the door of the hotel and began milling around the lobby, presenting hotel staff with the delicate question of what to do with them. Two security men tried to quiet them down—the question of throwing them out would depend on whether or not they were the children of hotel guests—but this only complicated the problem.

Howie, interpreting the iron grip on his shoulders as imminent danger, accidentally drop-kicked a vase, sending fragments of shattered pottery across the lush carpet. Sam, heroically rushing to his aid but blinded by his oversized sombrero, ran at full speed into a large potted fern, spraying dirt high into the air. This completely covered an elegantly dressed woman who was waiting for her escort to join her. He never made it across the lobby, for it was his destiny to trip over Sam's discarded sombrero and throw out his back. Nick disentangled himself from his Indian blanket and tossed it over the head of a security guard. Shocked, the man staggered a step backwards and fell with a tremendous splash into the lobby's ornate fountain. Sheldon, barely able to see the chaos beneath the low visor of his cap, attempted to run away but mistook a large mirrored wall for freedom. With a *crack,* he hit the wall, steel block first, and the image in front of him disintegrated into glass splinters at his feet.

Inside the casino there was a rush to the door to investigate the disturbance in the lobby. In the midst of the commotion Rob looked at Dennis. Dennis nodded—this might be their only chance. They ran up to the blackjack table and lifted Artie off the stool, one of them under each of his arms, then began to propel him through the crowd towards the exit.

"Hey!" yelled Butcher.

"Hey!" yelled the eight security men, who were under instructions to protect Artie from just such an assault.

Carrying Artie, Dennis and Rob attempted to plow through the crowd, using the attaché case—still firmly clutched in Artie's gloved hand—as a battering ram. They blasted into the lobby and froze at the sight of their five other campers, bizarrely dressed, scrambling around and knocking things over.

That momentary pause was their undoing. The eight security men fell on them from behind, knocking them sprawling and setting Artie free.

Chaos reigned. Dennis and Rob, not knowing which of their charges to rescue first, tried to wade through the teeming sea of people so they could be at the heart of the matter. But the eight security men pushed them aside as they rushed to find Artie. Voices rang out.

"What's going on?"

"Someone's trying to rob the old guy!"

"Someone's trying to *kidnap* the old guy!"

"Someone's trying to *murder* the old guy!"

"*Save the old guy!*"

"Who are all these kids?" screamed the desk clerk, desperately trying to calm down the woman who was covered with dirt from the upended fern.

"We're the Ambulance!" announced Kevin from underneath the end table he was using for cover.

The man who had tripped over the sombrero raised his head off the floor in agitation. "So what are you doing here—drumming up business?"

Just then Butcher staggered out of the casino. "Ambulance? Oh, no!"

The front door of the hotel burst open and the two federal agents ran inside, guns drawn.

"Newman, FBI!"

"Sheldon, Cow Expert!" announced Sheldon. He threw his arms wide to reveal his shirt, and the weight of the steel block became too much for one hand. Sixteen pounds of pure steel slipped from his grip and fell squarely on someone's foot.

"*Owww!*" cried Charlie Butcher, falling to the floor in pain.

Dennis leaned over his fallen boss. "Mr. Butcher, are you okay?"

Butcher blinked in confusion. "You know me? How do you know me?" He sat up and pointed an accusing finger at the counselor. "You're one of those Canadian Ambulance guys, and this is *all your fault!*"

"Quiet, everybody!" bellowed Newman. "This is a federal investigation! Calm down!"

"Save the old guy!" howled someone.

"*Who's* the old guy?" shouted O'Reilly. "This is the FBI! Order, everybody! Order!" The hubbub died down a little. Murmurs began to circulate.

"Hey, Harry, it's the FBI. Did we do anything lately?"

"Nah, they must've come for the old guy. I told

you nobody wins that much legally. He's cheating."

"Hey, I just heard the old guy cheats!"

"The old guy's a crook!"

"He's a menace to society!"

"*Kill the old guy!*"

One of the casino security men grabbed Rob by the collar. "You and your friend tried to make off with the old guy. Who is he to you, anyway?"

"He's—he's—he's our grandfather," Rob stammered.

The two FBI agents moved through the crowd and climbed up on top of the hotel desk, which afforded them the best view of the lobby. "Quiet!" bawled Newman. The murmurs died. "Now, listen. I want the guys who belong to this Juniortours group Ambulance to step forward."

Dennis, Rob and the five campers disentangled themselves from the crowd and began to thread their way through the people towards the two agents at the desk.

Newman spoke. "I make it five kids, and you're supposed to have six."

"Well," began Rob, "you see, our sixth kid—that is, the old guy is really—uh—Artie is—oh, forget it. Arrest me."

"So you're the one who's behind all these kid-in-the-tuxedo scams?" prompted O'Reilly.

Rob's head jerked up. "The kid in the tuxedo? You mean, you know about the kid in the tuxedo? Well, he's—he's—oh my God, where is he?"

"Where's the old guy?" called someone.

"The old guy isn't here!"

"The old guy is missing!"

"He's escaped!"

"*Get the old guy!*"

The mob, ignited once again, burst out the front door of the hotel in time to see Artie, sprinting with surprising agility for a man his age, leap a hedge, jump into a cab and speed off.

"Stop that kid!" shouted Rob.

"What kid?" called O'Reilly.

"That old man is our sixth kid! He's the one who always wears the tuxedo, and he's *eleven years old!*"

The crowd surged and boiled under the bright lights of the Strip.

"After him!" cried someone, and there was a great rush to the parking lot.

Ambulance group forgotten, Newman and O'Reilly leapt into their illegally-parked car and roared off in the direction the taxi had taken. Cars poured out of the Gunhold lot and followed the FBI men as the casino patrons rushed to see the elderly cheater brought to justice.

* * *

Artie got out of the taxi at McCarron International Airport, paid the driver and darted into the building and up to the information desk.

"When's the next flight to Canada, please?"

The girl looked at him oddly. His voice did not match his face. "Where in Canada, sir?"

"Anywhere, please, just so it leaves soon."

She checked the departure list. "American Airlines has one going to Toronto in five minutes, but I don't think you'll have time to—"

174

Artie darted down to the American Airlines desk, bought his ticket, threw his money at the clerk in a green blur of cash, and raced through the screening procedure. He arrived at the gate gasping for breath just as the flight attendant announced, "Last call."

Soon he was comfortably established in his seat and the plane began to taxi towards the runway. Suddenly it stopped. The intercom crackled on, but instead of the usual announcements there was a long pause.

Finally a voice said: *Ladies and gentlemen, we have been recalled to the gate. Nothing is wrong, and we apologize for the delay.*

* * *

At the end of the loading ramp, waiting for the DC-8 to return, stood Newman and O'Reilly, two airport police officers, Dennis, Rob and Butcher. All the other people—the five boys, the eight security men and the interested observers—were assigned to a waiting room on the Arrivals level.

The sleek nose of the plane appeared, then the aircraft aligned itself with the gate. The door was opened, and the seven men filed inside. Artie was not in his assigned seat, but one of the washrooms was occupied.

Rob knocked lightly on the door. "Artie, is that you?"

There was no answer.

"Artie, we know it's you," called Newman, "so you might as well open up. The game is definitely over."

There was a *click* and the bathroom door opened to reveal Artie Geller, his disguise gone without a trace, dressed in the jeans and short-sleeved shirt he had worn to Hoover Dam that afternoon.

The two FBI men started at the sight of him. This was the felon, the confidence man, the fleeing fugitive? This *child*?

Artie said, "Hi, Dennis. Hi, Rob."

"You're under arrest," O'Reilly managed, feeling foolish. Quickly he sped through the list of Artie's rights.

"And now, young fellow," said Newman, "I'll take that briefcase."

Artie stepped back, ripped open his shirt, reached into the leather pouch and came up with the gold key. He popped it into his mouth and swallowed.

Every muscle of Newman's body seemed to slump. "Aw, kid, no! Aw, no, no, *no!*" He turned to O'Reilly, his face registering panic. "Tim, where's the nearest hospital around here?"

Butcher, who had not made it past the First Class section, suddenly said, "Hey, a plane! I'm taking a trip!" He turned clumsily to the nearest passenger. "Where are we going?"

"Toronto," said the man.

Butcher recoiled. "Toronto? But that's—that's in *Canada!*" The tour director's body went limp and he crumpled to the floor, dead to the world.

Coins

The doctor held the x-ray up to the light for Newman and O'Reilly to view. "I'm telling you, gentlemen, there is no key inside this boy."

"But we saw him swallow it," O'Reilly protested. "It has to be in there."

"Well, it's not," said the doctor. "Pure and simple."

Newman turned to Artie. "Kid, where's the key?"

Artie shrugged.

"Look, Artie, if you don't give us the key we're not going to send you home with the briefcase and forget the whole thing. We're going to pry it open or shoot it open or blast it open. It's up to you. We don't care, but it's your case."

Artie nodded in resignation. He reached into his mouth, drew out the key, wiped it carefully on his pants and handed it over. The two agents stared.

Newman hefted the attaché case onto a counter, unlocked it and lifted the lid. The shocked silence that followed was punctuated only by the sound of breaking glass as a passing nurse glanced at the stacks of bills and dropped a tray of test tubes.

"Oh!" groaned the doctor. "If that was mine, *I* would have swallowed the key!"

* * *

Dennis and Rob were sent back to the trailer park with their five campers. Artie went with Newman and O'Reilly and the confiscated attaché case to an elegant suite of rooms in the agents' hotel. There he was confined to a room while the two FBI men tried to figure out what to do with him.

In custody one Arthur Geller, known as "the kid in the tuxedo," sometimes called "A," an eleven-year-old Canadian citizen participating in the Ju-niortours touring program—certainly not the sort of thing the FBI would want to see go to trial. Their superiors would say, "So you're telling us that this kid did all those things by himself? What do you think we are—stupid?" The press would say, "That's right—pick on an eleven-year-old kid while gangsters and murderers roam the streets." The public would say, "Awww, the poor little guy!" The Canadian government would protest, the American government would apologize, Newman and O'Reilly would come out the villains, and everyone would forget that Artie had done anything wrong at all. He would immediately become a folk hero, probably with a host of imitators—hundreds of children following his trail to success. The implications were staggering.

Besides, both Newman and O'Reilly felt that it

wouldn't be right to throw the book at a bright little guy like Artie. Even though he had violated an incredible number of laws, his schemes had never really hurt anyone.

After five hours of work without sleep the two FBI men summoned Dennis and Rob to be with Artie when the Bureau's decision was handed down. The meeting took place around a long glass coffee table in the agents' suite.

"Now," Newman began, "this is an official hearing which is completely off the record—which, I suppose, makes it an unofficial hearing. But in view of the extenuating circumstances, and in order to avoid adverse publicity..." He stopped and gazed at them honestly. "Look, I'm not a diplomat. What I'm trying to say is that this whole thing would make everybody look really bad if too many people found out about it." He swallowed. "Okay, the suspect is charged with the following: in New York, New York, selling without a license, false advertising, contravention of FDA standards and violation of state sales tax laws; in Washington, D.C., running an illegal gaming house, misuse of public property, inciting to riot and littering; at the Lake McConaughy State Recreation Area, Nebraska, defacing public property, bringing livestock into a state park without a permit, operating a dairy without proper health inspection, operating a store without a license, operating a commercial enterprise on state property without a permit, selling unpasteurized milk in unsanitary containers, involving minors in an illegal operation and evasion of state taxes; in Denver, Colorado, appropriation of a private building without permission, subsequently causing approximately twenty-eight hundred cases of trespassing, performance of unauthorized alterations on said building, failure to pay electric, water and telephone bills incurred, selling food and liquor without a license, price-fixing, operating a discotheque without a license, violation of local fire marshall's laws, maintaining a salaried staff without withholding appropriate tax and social security deductions, violation of state advertising laws, littering, disturbing the peace, numerous counts of generally immoral business practises and evasion of state taxes; in Las Vegas, Nevada, gambling underage, leaving the scene of a crime and attempting to flee the country. In addition to all this there's total failure to pay federal income tax and responsibility for all damages to the Las Vegas Hotel Gunhold incurred in the events leading up to capture, including the cost of two abdominal x-rays." Newman breathed deeply. "Tim, could you get me a glass of water, please?"

Dennis and Rob looked sick; Artie's face was impassive.

Newman drank deeply and wiped the sweat from his forehead. "Now, what we want to do is about halfway between justice and a cover-up. We're willing to forget—well, maybe not forget—but forgive the whole thing, provided you, Artie, make total restitution. That is, we'll take off federal income tax and state taxes, the price of every license and permit you didn't have, all the pertinent fines—and there are a few—your unpaid bills and reparations to the Hotel Gunhold and the Twister Pretzel Company. And"—he held up his hand—"before we give you a chance to respond to that, I'd better tell you that if you don't accept our terms we intend to press charges to the fullest. Now, do we have a deal?"

"Deal," said Artie so quickly that it startled Dennis and Rob.

"Good," said Newman. "And it just so happens that we've worked it all out in advance. You owe us $149,764.04." He thrust a fifteen-foot-long computer print-out onto the table. "Feel free to check the calculations."

Dennis leapt to his feet. "Be reasonable! Where's Artie going to get a hundred and fifty thousand dollars?"

"From his briefcase, that's where!" Newman snapped right back. From under the table he produced the attaché case and slammed it down in front of Artie. "And here's his change!" Newman slumped back in his chair, fuming.

"Now," he added, cooling off somewhat, "in the interests of avoiding the biggest mess you've ever seen—and let me tell you, deportation hearings are a pain in the neck—I've decided to let you finish the tour. I'm assuming you've got the brains not to pull any more of this stuff. We'll be watching you."

O'Reilly spoke up. "Artie, I hope you realize how lucky you are that Agent Newman isn't pressing charges."

"Thank you very much, sir," said Artie.

Rob allowed himself to breathe again. "Thanks from me too!"

"Don't thank me," said Newman wearily. "Just keep an eye on *him* from now on."

Artie opened the attaché case and counted his

money. There was $77.96. Between New York and Las Vegas he had turned a net profit of $2.96. His usually impassive face evidenced slight distaste—coins.

* * *

For some reason Rob expected that now things would be different for Ambulance group, but everything was the same. When Dennis, Rob and Artie left the hotel the *click* they heard signified that yet another moment had been captured on film for Kevin's growing photo collection. Rob could only guess how this one would be catalogued:

Roll 5000, exposure 1. Dennis, Rob and Artie after dropping $150,000 in big FBI investigation.

Howie complained that the city of Las Vegas neglected astronomy to a shameful degree. Sam got into a fight at the campground and started a two-hour debate on human rights and liberties as pertaining to the game of Red Rover. Nick announced his intention of staying away from Sheldon for the next seven years because of the broken mirror at the Hotel Gunhold. Sheldon borrowed a tape recorder and began work on a ninety-minute cassette to mail to Pete Ogrodnick in Finland. The tape was filled with endless rapturous details about the adventures of Ambulance group. (Poor Pete, Rob thought, would probably be just as sick of hearing about Ambulance group as Ambulance group was of hearing about Pete.) Dennis bought a large hat with a full-size operational roulette wheel on the crown.

Nothing had changed. It was almost comforting.

Artie seemed the least affected of anyone, as though he were not at all perturbed at the loss of a hundred and fifty thousand dollars and a close brush with federal agents.

Rob smiled at the memory of the evening after the FBI incident. "What did you want all that money for anyway?" he had asked Artie.

The familiar shrug. "Nothing."

Nothing! Rob would never again be able to hear that word without flinching. Artie had put his mark on it forever. It was now, quite literally, *nothing*.

Watching Kevin thread yet another film into his camera, Rob sat back with a sigh. In the distance he could hear Butcher yelling at something or someone. Ambulance group had seen neither hide nor hair of Butcher since the big night in Las Vegas—he seemed to be avoiding them. Dennis called this new circumstance "establishing rapport with the boss." Rob had to laugh. It looked as if this explosive tour, which had blown up in his face at frequent intervals, was going to die a peaceful death.

* * *

At the Los Angeles trailer park Dennis and Rob stayed up late, sitting around the campfire, endearing themselves to the Lillies of the Valley, two counselors who, according to Dennis, "make all those other girls look like men." Dennis never gave up.

In the Ambulance tent Nick was reciting the

gross misfortunes that befall those who break mirrors. No one was interested, with the possible exception of Sheldon, who was getting scared.

Artie sat up. "According to my tour book, almost seven and a half million people live in and around Los Angeles."

"Yeah?" prompted Sam expectantly.

"A city that size is bound to have its problems with crime," Artie went on thoughtfully. "Its citizens deserve protection, both on the street and in the home. But . . . "

All five listeners sat up and looked at Artie eagerly.

"But I'm under surveillance. Which is a shame."

"We could help you!" blurted Howie. "We're not under surveillance!"

"You mean you'd be willing to do this for me?"

"Sure!" chorused everybody.

"Well, I guess we're partners then," said Artie briskly. "Tomorrow morning, Sheldon, you get the jelly . . . "